Running Hot

Running Hot

A BAD BOYS UNDERCOVER NOVELLA

HELENKAY DIMON

AVONIMPULSE
An Imprint of HarperCollinsPublishers

Excerpt from *Playing Dirty* copyright © 2015 by HelenKay Dimon.

Excerpt from *An Heiress for All Seasons* copyright © 2014 by Sharie Kohler.

Excerpt from *Intrusion* copyright © 2014 by Charlotte Stein.

Excerpt from *Can't Wait* copyright © 2013 by Jennifer Hopkins. This novella originally appeared in the anthology *All I Want for Christmas Is a Cowboy.*

Excerpt from *The Laws of Seduction* copyright © 2014 by Gwen T. Weerheim-Jones.

Excerpt from *Sinful Rewards 1* copyright © 2014 by Cynthia Sax.

Excerpt from *Sweet Cowboy Christmas* copyright © 2014 by Candis Terry.

EPub Edition DECEMBER 2014 ISBN: 9780062357823

Print Edition ISBN: 9780062357830

AM 10 9 8 7 6 5 4 3 2 1

For Wendy Duren,
my inspiration for a heroine
who is the perfect blend of beautiful and fierce.

Chapter One

WARD BENNETT JERKED back into consciousness. One shift, and he nearly wrenched his shoulder out of its socket. He didn't need to see the plastic zip tie to know that's what dug into his wrists and bound them behind his back.

Moving his ankle, he didn't meet any resistance. The person who shackled him had made a pretty big miscalculation. As if he needed his hands to escape. Any idiot could break a zip tie. But first he had to figure out how he'd gotten in this position and why.

That must have been one hell of a date. It was a fucking shame he couldn't remember one minute of it.

Humidity made his skin slick, and sweat gathered between his shoulder blades as he scanned the open area. He'd been in similar structures for a week now but didn't recognize this particular one. He'd call it a bungalow or cabana of sorts. The locals referred to it as a bure.

Wooden beams, a thatched straw ceiling soaring a good twenty feet above his head, open walls, and not a stick of furniture other than the chair he was tied to.

A warm breeze blew over him, and darkness fell around him on all sides. He could make out the shadow of trees and smell the ocean in the distance. He strained to listen for the usual sounds of the resort—the mumble of conversation and ever-present local music piped through the speakers, maybe the sound of motorboats in the distance—but heard nothing.

People described this place as paradise. Right now, to him, Fiji pretty much sucked.

As soon as the thought registered, footsteps echoed around him. The gentle sway of hips came into view. His gaze traveled up the tanned, lean legs peeking out from under the navy cargo shorts. Then to the sliver of bare stomach visible at the bottom of the slim tank top and to the impressive breasts filling out the top of it. He finally landed on that face.

Tasha Gregory, the damn-she's-hot, smooth-talking bartender from the Waitui Resort. The same one with the husky voice that made him stupid. From the slight wave in her long blond hair to the big brown eyes, everything about her worked for him. Which was how they ended up at her place last night…but the rest between then and now was a blur.

The "how" was simple enough to understand. The zipping attraction had led to flirting. That explained why he'd spent most of the last six nights parked on a stool across from her, trading bits of island gossip. Well, that and because he was on Maku, a private island in the pacific nation of Fiji, to gather intel. She just happened to be a smokin' hot source of intel.

Which led to a new issue. For a supposed resort bartender she sure knew her way around a zip tie. And he was not an easy man to get the jump on. He'd been trained by the best at the Farm, the CIA's top-secret training facility near Williamsburg, Virginia. There he'd learned how to do everything from survive interrogation to fly a helicopter to cut a man's head off, sometimes all at the same time.

A hundred-twenty-pound hottie shouldn't worry him, but he'd lived long enough to appreciate the power of a pissed-off female. And he seemed to have ticked this one off in a big way. Normally not a problem, but he had a job to do and being tied to a chair made that tough.

He twisted his hands, trying to keep the rest of his arms still and not give away his movements as he inched his thumb closer to his back jeans pocket. "Uh, Tasha?"

"You're awake."

He still wasn't clear on when and how he'd gone to sleep. "You don't seem too happy about that."

"Not really." She didn't bother to look up as she shuffled her way through his wallet, picking out one item at a time, checking it then letting it drop to the floor by her feet.

Again, not exactly the usual bartender MO. Of course, every item on the floor could pass for real but wasn't. His cover depended on that level of craftsmanship.

He cleared his throat. "This is not the way I generally end a date. Start one, sure, but not end."

"Shut up." She exhaled as she dumped the rest of the wallet on the floor and slipped a phone out of her back pocket.

"Now, that phrase I've heard on dates." His eyes narrowed as he realized the cell she held looked an awful lot like his burner. "Care to tell me what we're doing?"

She finally glanced up, firing a load of you're-a-dead-man fury in his direction. "Who are you?"

There was a question he couldn't answer. The CIA tended to frown on black ops agents spilling their biographical data. She could pull out a flamethrower and put it to his dick and he'd still duck this one. And he was starting to worry she had a lethal weapon of some sort on her.

"I thought we dealt with that days ago. I came to the bar. You served me drinks. We've been flirting and then we graduated to touching." Sweet Jesus, the touching. She had smooth skin and this body that was so fit and curvy it made his fucking eyes cross. "Any of this sound familiar?"

"We're done playing games." That's all she said. Dropped the comment, and then nothing.

She stood eight feet away, outside of kicking distance, and didn't move. No telltale signs of nerves. She didn't shift her weight or her gaze. She looked at him as if she could kick his ass and was just seconds away from starting. For some reason, Ward found that sexy as hell.

The fact she'd dropped her usual smile and now came off as trained and not some random bartender was not quite as sexy. A grifter maybe? A hot woman who conned men out of their vacation money. Possible.

Thinking she might have a partner, Ward glanced to the side. The kick of pain had him blinking and swearing. Looked like he couldn't move his head without bringing on a stabbing sensation. That was new. "My head is killing me. What the hell kind of sex did we have?"

"None."

Well, that was a damn shame. "Is that why you tied me up? Because I'm totally capable. I assure you. We can go right now."

"You talk too much." But she stepped in closer.

He'd been accused of a lot of shit on this job. Being chatty was not one. "You're not exactly coughing up information here."

"Nor will I."

"You were more fun as a bartender." Her arm shot out so fast he almost didn't twist away in time. In and out. One shot, then she backed up again. Not that he could get too far while stuck in the chair or do anything to grab her anyway. At the last minute he threw his head to the side and took the brunt of the smack from the heel of her hand on his collarbone instead of his chin. Good thing, since his head ached enough already. "Damn, woman, that hurt."

"It was supposed to."

Felt like she held a weight in her hand or something. "Then congratulations."

"This isn't funny, and you're no tourist."

That made them even, as there was no way that hit came from a novice. Still, if she wanted to play, they'd play. "I'm a businessman."

"A financial planner. Yeah, you fed me that line days ago."

"What, you're not a fan of money?" It was a good cover. Solid. On business in New Zealand before he flew over for a vacation detour. Getting some sun, relaxing... maybe finding a hot bartender.

"Actually, I hate liars."

This was not going well. Hard to charm a woman who looked ready to kill him, but he tried anyway. "Maybe you could untie me."

She pulled a gun out from behind her back. Not a baby gun either. No, this was a SIG Sauer P229, the same type that he preferred to carry and could put a good-sized hole in him.

He cleared his throat. "Or not."

"Your record is clean." She took a step closer. Just one and not quite far enough.

"I don't know what that means." But he did. She was talking in a language he knew all too well. In an instant he went from thinking about her as some kind of con woman looking to score on a hapless businessman to something very different. Something mercenary and potentially dangerous to his operation.

"The underage drinking charge was a nice touch on your record. Most people clean up their backgrounds a bit too much." She shot him a level gaze. "But I think you know that."

Forget mercenary. This woman worked for someone. Getting that deep into his cover, past the stuff that even though faked should have looked as if it were expunged, meant connections. Impressive ones. "And you know this as part of your job as a resort bartender?"

"Yes."

"Now who's lying?" He focused on her face as he slipped the homemade shim out of his back pocket and went to work forcing it under the locking mechanism on the zip tie.

The who-was-she possibilities spun through his head. He was there on a sanctioned job to find a nasty dictator hiding in paradise. The operation's directive was clear: find Drissa Tigana and neutralize him before he started selling off some of those rocket launchers he'd stolen when he skipped his country and headed here. Fear was Tigana would destabilize Fiji, and no one wanted that to happen except possibly Tigana.

Tasha could be one more person looking to make a quick buck in Fiji. Ward leaned toward believing that possibility but wondered if maybe he'd stumbled into something unrelated to Tigana. Maybe she liked tying guys up. Any way you looked at it, their time together was about done, which was a damn shame since they'd skipped the sex part.

Her gaze bounced away from his face then returned. "You're not as smooth as you think you are."

"I refuse to believe that's true." But just in case, he stopped fiddling behind his back.

"You're not as attractive as you think either." She took another step.

"Come on now. Take that back." He judged the distance between them. Another few inches and he'd take her down. Might even feel bad about it for a few seconds, despite the fact she'd tied him to a chair.

"And that thing you're doing…" She eyed him up.

Interesting, but she was going to need to be more specific since he had about ten exit strategies swimming around in his head at the moment. "Being charming?"

"You're counting my steps and thinking, 'Wow, she was too dumb to tie my feet to the chair,' and are now spinning all kinds of plans about getting the jump on me."

Well, shit. "I have no idea what you're talking about. I sit at a desk all day."

"You should know, if you move your feet even one inch I will punch you in the junk so hard I'll have to send an apology to the future kids you'll never have." She winked at him. "Got that, stud?"

Sweet hell. Enemy or not, mercenary or con woman, she was so fucking hot. "You have my attention."

"Then tell me your name."

"Ward Bennett."

She sighed. "Your real name."

He wedged the shim under the tie's locking bar and tugged. If she'd bound his hands together in front of him, he'd be out and knocking her down already. "You think if I made one up I'd go with that?"

"Since you won't talk when I'm being nice—"

"This is you being nice?" He snorted for effect and to cover any noise from behind his back. "I gotta tell you, sweetheart. Your dating etiquette needs work."

"We'll do this the hard way." As she said the words, the gun came up again until it aimed at his head.

"Lower that." At this distance, she should be able to hit some body part he needed, and that was not okay with him.

"Then talk."

He thought about keeping up the businessman ruse and doing a whole fake panic song and dance, but she clearly didn't buy the cover. No need to act like an idiot and give her even more reason to blow his nuts off. "Give me a topic and I'll babble until your damn head falls off, but put the weapon away."

"This is your last chance."

"Who do you think I am?" He slammed his foot against the floor to throw off her concentration as he took one last whack at the zip tie.

"No, we're not doing it that way."

She sure as hell talked like someone with intelligence experience. He mentally ran through the briefings for this operation. No one came to the island except him and Ford Decker, who was currently pretending to be a wealthy entrepreneur looking to buy a private Fijian island of his own. Up until ten minutes ago, Ward thought by hanging out with Tasha every night he got the better end of this op, but now he envied Ford and his task of sucking up to the idiot resort owner.

The island consisted of one all-inclusive resort and a few bures for the people who worked there. In a space that size they couldn't afford to bring in a team of people. They'd streamlined, and now Ward wondered if they'd gone a bit too bare bones; something else was clearly at play on Maku, and it looked like Tasha might be in the middle of it.

"I'm guessing since you have the gun and the sudden can-kick-your-ass scary-woman thing happening that you're not a regular bartender." He didn't usually point out the obvious, but he needed to stall for a bit more time.

"You think?"

That was the closest she came to admitting anything. Her background check had been clean. He had her file memorized. A California girl who landed in Fiji after washing out of college in Hawaii. She had the surfer girl look, but suddenly nothing else in the backstory fit as neatly as it once did.

"Look, I don't care who you are. And if you're into weapons during foreplay, more power to you. But it's time to let me go, Tasha. I check out of this place in two days and head back to my boring life. So, I want to enjoy the island before I leave."

"I'm going to shoot you in the knee in three seconds." She aimed, and the frown suggested she wasn't bluffing. "One..."

"Ward Bennett."

"Two..."

Damn if she didn't look spitting angry and ready to fire. "You forgot one thing."

"What?"

"Any idiot can defeat a zip tie." One yank of his hands, and he heard the rip. The tie dropped to the floor, and his arms fell to his sides.

He was up and out of the chair in a second, ignoring the rattling in his head. She jumped back, but he moved faster. He nailed her in the midsection, thinking he'd take her to the floor and question her once he had her pinned down and under him.

She tried to stop him with a knee to the jaw, but he held on. With one hand under her knee, he tugged, and her balance faltered. He started to knock her down when he felt the prick in his shoulder.

That fast, his fingers stopped bending and he lost his hold. Before he could shout, his tongue went numb and his muscles turned to liquid. One second he was on his feet, and the next he slammed to his knees. He could feel his body lean from one side to the other as he stared at the floor, watching the wood slats jump and dance through blurred vision.

Gentle hands pushed him onto his side. Her hair swept over her shoulder and against his cheek as she leaned over him. No matter how hard he tried, how much he concentrated, he couldn't reach out and grab her. He didn't even have enough control over his body to shove her away when her lips brushed against his ear.

"And you forgot that I knocked you out once." She waved something in front of his face. Looked like a needle. "Lucky for me I brought a second dose."

The bure started to spin.

"Be a good boy and stay out of my way, Ward."

Chapter Two

As FAR AS great escapes went, Tasha thought she'd pulled off that one pretty well.

She jogged through the rough terrain, over the tree roots, and dove into the thick groupings of trees. Her hiking boots slid over the fallen branches made wet from the just-after-dawn humidity. After a few minutes of blocking every thought and concentrating on staying on her feet, she broke through the brush and into the small clearing. A beat-up, fifteen-year-old SUV waited for her in the prearranged space by the dock on the far side of the three-hundred-acre island.

She lowered the tailgate and lifted the torn carpet over the floorboard. After a quick press of the code into the lock, she heard a click and the hidden drawer popped open. She scanned the cache of shiny weapons stored inside before trading the gun strapped to her side for two knives. This part of the assignment called for weapons she could hide on her body without tipping off the local police.

There were very few easy afternoons as an officer for the Secret Intelligence Service, otherwise known as Britain's MI6, but Tasha found today especially annoying. She'd lost contact with the other officer on the ground in Fiji, hated the reports coming from the home office about Tigana…and then there was the Ward issue.

The guy was a complete pain in the ass. Hot in that one-smoky-look-could-burn-away-your-underwear type of way, but a nuisance. She should have known he'd be trouble when he'd sauntered up to her bar, all tall and sexy and full of self-confidence. Between the full mouth and the muscular swimmer's body, he'd had her common sense flickering.

She blamed too many days on the job. Too much heat. His slim-fitting T-shirts…

Thanks to the hottie with the light brown hair and intense brown eyes, she had a mess on her hands. Looked like Ward was not a simple businessman. Not a simple anything. A gun-for-hire maybe.

Just fantastic.

The only way to remove Ward as a threat had been with a mix of sex and drugs. Men fell for that double whammy every single time, but men like Ward only fell once. She wouldn't get that shot again.

But thinking about the big guy dropping to the floor did make her smile. Also made her grab a gun, just to be safe. She tucked it into her boot before closing up the Jeep again. Now came the long hike through the overgrown jungle. This Fijian island, one of more than three hundred excluding the hundreds more islets that made up the country, was more remote than most. Its residents included people who worked at the resort, tourists, and one very nasty dictator with some stolen big guns. The egotistical jackass.

She walked half a mile, baking in the island humidity and generally soaking through her shirt until a chill played on her skin. She'd given up on the rocky trail. More like, it ran out and she took to the brush, using one of her knives to clear a path.

Halfway from nowhere, or so the GPS on her watch suggested, she heard scuffling. She'd ignored the patter and slither of whatever moved around her so far, but this sounded human. Male, human, and loud.

No way was she taking the risk of running into the wrong group of men out here alone. She knew she could take them, but that meant blowing her cover and possibly letting the wrong people know operatives were at work on the island.

She looked around for a place to hide and didn't see so much as a hole to dive into. Ducking down, she peeked through the wooded area and saw heavily armed men walking in the distance about three hundred meters to her left. Men she didn't recognize.

She had only seconds.

Edging her back around the tree trunk, she moved along the ground until she found a branch she could grab. One just out of reach. With her weapons tucked in her shorts, she did a standing jump. On the first attempt, her palm slapped against the rough bark, and she bit back a hiss.

Focusing all her energy, she tried again, this time snagging the branch with the tips of her fingers. One hand up. Then the next. With a deep breath, she lifted her body up until her stomach rested on the bark. Next came the leg swing and the scramble higher and deeper into the tree.

From her position sitting among the leaves, she could watch and maybe drop on any potential attackers. Or wait. Tasha knew how to bide her time. She possessed a wealth of patience and willingness to shoot if needed. But she could wait only so long because Tigana was on the move and Ward was out there somewhere, likely planning his revenge.

She'd almost rather take her chances with Tigana.

WARD HEARD THE footsteps. Not the light touch of a female. No, this thumped with no thought to hiding a presence.

He tried to open his eyes, get his bearings. He remembered the pain in his head from before. Right after he had the thought, the hammering started hard enough to make his eyes cross. Tasha, damn her. She drugged him. Knocked him out cold and left him.

He tried to move his arms and felt the now-familiar tug of a binding holding them behind his back. "Son of a bitch."

He blinked again and this time spied shoes. Well-worn sneakers, to be exact.

The floor creaked, and Ford Decker's face came into view as he squatted on his haunches next to Ward's head. "Hello there."

All Ward could manage was a groan. Yeah, a *son of a bitch* wasn't nearly strong enough for this scene. Having a witness, especially *this* witness, made him long to be unconscious again.

"I guess it's a lucky thing you had a tracker on you," Ford said.

"Yeah, I feel lucky right now."

Ford's hand hung down between his knees, and he let out a long whistle. "So, how did the date go?"

Instead of answering, Ward closed his eyes again. "Shit."

"You often end a night of sex tied to a chair? I had no idea you were into funky shit." Ford snorted. "In fact, I kind of wish I didn't know it now."

Ward let his senses race. He felt the hard wood under his legs and the floor pressing into his side. The chair. She actually took the time to strap him to the chair. "She did it again."

It was a message of some sort. One Ward didn't get, but he planned to track her down and ask her.

"Did you say again?" The laughter was right there in Ford's voice.

Yeah, that was just about all the amusement Ward could handle for one day. "Shut up."

Ford barked out an actual laugh that time. "Oh, I don't see that happening."

With only one eye open but squinting against the morning light filling the bure, Ward glanced over at his partner on this operation. "You could help me get up."

"Or I could take a photo." Ford took a phone out of his pocket as if he intended to go through with it.

"Do and die." Tied up or not, a chair or not, if Ford walked out of the room with one piece of evidence about this and the shitty night that came before, Ward would take him apart. There were limits on how much bashing his ego could handle.

"Answer this." Ford picked up Ward's abandoned wallet and flipped it around. "Did you have a good time, or were you so bad she tied you up to get away from you?"

There was only one answer to that sort of question. "Fuck you."

"That's not really responsive."

Time to get the assignment back on track and Ford's mind off whatever happened before he walked into this room. Not that Ward even knew the answer. But they did have a problem, and he was clear on at least that much. "She's not a bartender."

Ford's smirk vanished. "What is she?"

"Con woman. Operative. Mercenary." Ward tried to lift up, to take the weight off his sore shoulder. "Hell, an actress for all I know."

"That's a lot of skill sets for one woman."

He struggled up to his elbow. The awkward position made it tough to break a tie a second time but at least he felt a bit more in control of his surroundings. "I don't know who she really is. Our intel didn't go deep enough."

Ford shook his head as he jumped to his feet and started walking around the open room, scooping up the contents of Ward's wallet off the floor as he went. "Man, you know how to pick them."

Turning his wrists, Ward realized the way his hands were bound provided some give. He couldn't slip them out, but it wouldn't take that much strength to rip the tie apart. Especially since Ford didn't seem all that inclined to help perform a rescue.

"She is hot." The comment slipped out, but Ward decided it needed to be said. Maybe as an explanation for losing his grip. Maybe because he couldn't forget her face.

Ford hummed. "Smokin', yeah."

"She also carries weapons and, as you can see, went through my wallet."

"Then there's the part where she dropped you to the ground like a rag doll. You, a complete hardass with hundreds of thousands of dollars of training behind you." Ford held out the wallet in front of Ward's face. "That's just sad, man."

Ward wanted to grab it. Would have if he could move his hands. "Did you miss the part where I said 'fuck you'?"

"It would be easier to take you seriously if you weren't tied to a chair."

The smartass comment got Ward moving. He shifted his hand, turned, and…snap. "There. I'm free."

Ford shrugged. "Better, but still embarrassing."

"Thanks for your support." Ward rubbed his wrists as he sat up.

"You know I plan on telling everyone we know about this, right?"

With his head still spinning and his ego deflating with each passing second, Ward jumped to his feet. "I'll stab you and leave you for dead on the island."

"Gotta be honest. You're not that scary to me right now." Ford walked over to the edge of the bure and scanned the tropical forest beyond. "Tasha weighs, what, a buck-thirty?"

"If that." Thinking about her brought a flash of her face to Ward's mind. Damn if she didn't have him wrapped around and chasing his own ass.

Ford was right about one thing: this situation was pretty damn embarrassing.

Ford turned back with his hands on his hips and a stupid grin on his mouth. "She took you down without trouble, so I'm betting I could take you without working up a sweat."

"Tough talk, but you didn't see her." The legs, that ass...the sexy way she held her own, not even a little afraid of him. Ward shook his head to push those thoughts out and stay focused. "Or the big needle she hit me with."

"Interesting."

Ward held up two fingers. "Twice."

"She drugged you multiple times, but you still think she's hot." Ford mumbled something under his breath. Something about Ward being a dumbass.

"Hell, yeah."

"You sick bastard." Ford took an extra gun out from where he had it tucked behind his back and handed it to

Ward. Added in a lot of head shaking and a few more "dumbass" comments as he went. "Now what?"

"We go after her." More out of habit than anything else, Ward checked the weapon. Satisfied it would do the job until he could get his hands on one of the stashes he had hidden around the island, he held it. He was ready to fight, and he had a feeling a battle loomed right around the corner—and not just with Tasha.

Ford used the toe of his sneaker to move the remaining debris around the floor. Broken zip ties and scattered papers. Nothing of any value, but all of it out of place in this out-of-the-way locale.

"We have three hundred acres to cover. Want to point me in the right direction?" he asked.

"She's wherever you think Tigana is." Call it instinct, but Ward knew. Tasha was not on the island for sightseeing or to make a few bucks. She had a job to do. Just like him.

Ford froze. "You really think she's here to get to him?"

No question. "This is going to be a race to see who gets to the guy first, and it's going to be us."

"But she could still mess up our operation."

Ward could almost hear the pieces click together in Ford's brain. The operation goals were clear. Go in, take Tigana out, and secure the weapons. No room for error. No way to take on the responsibility of a random woman on the island…regardless of how good she looked in those cargo shorts. "Definitely."

"Damn." Ford shook his head. "I hate this assignment."

"At least no one drugged you." The woman could have at least kissed him first. Seemed obvious to Ward.

"As if you didn't enjoy it."

Ward hated to admit it, but his partner was not wrong on that score. He never thought of himself as the punishment type, but the whole kick-ass thing Tasha had going on worked for him. On every pathetic level.

"Oh, I intend to talk with Tasha about her nasty needle habit when I find her." That and the flirting and the touching. Maybe see how they could get back there when the assignment ended.

"Plan on sticking it to her, do you?" Ford managed to ask the question with a straight face.

No way could Ward answer without sounding like a complete jackass. Not usually something that worried him, but he'd long grown out of the whole prove-your-dick-size-with-raunchy-locker-room-talk thing.

Ford broke the silence with what amounted to more of his unending commentary. "I'm just asking because you need to stay on task."

That one Ward could not ignore. "Meaning?"

"The hot bartender isn't our assignment."

Red-hot temper whipped up out of nowhere, and Ward shoved it back. "I know what the job is. I'm in charge, remember?"

Ford glanced at the ripped zip tie and the overturned chair. "Yeah, you look like you've got this handled."

Chapter Three

A WOMAN COULD only sit in a tree for so long before the whole thing got silly. After three hours of waiting and watching, Tasha stretched. The branches bent and the leaves swayed as she balanced her leg along the bark. The soft, warm breeze caught most of the noise, but the right person, a trained person, might sense or hear her presence.

The muscles in her legs ached, and her finger cramped in its position along the side of her knife. She switched off from ready position to surveillance for about the hundredth time since she'd crawled up there. The small, lightweight binoculars were infrared and long range. She'd rather have a muffin, but they did have a practical use.

She scanned the trees. The ground. The distance.

Nothing. A strange lack of nothing.

The newest mumble of voices had disappeared fifteen minutes ago, and the sun burned through the trees, casting part of the forest floor in white spotlights and the rest in shadows. Not the best place to hide, but then again she didn't pick this battlefield.

After a few seconds of moving her legs and making sure her body parts still worked, she gathered her few possessions and dropped to the ground. Her knees bore the impact, as did the palm she balanced against the earth where she landed.

She took two steps before her senses clicked into high alert. A noise—slight, almost silent—passed by her left side. It was little more than a whisper of air, but she knew what that meant.

Before she could turn around, something hard pressed into the back of her head. The barrel of a gun. "Damn it."

"Hello, sunshine."

She'd know that husky voice anywhere. It licked against her in her dreams. Played in her head long after he'd abandoned his seat across from her at the bar during all those nights.

Ward Bennett.

She should have shot him and been done with it. So much for wanting to preserve his hot face with that bit of scruff and those meet-me-in-the-bedroom eyes.

She started to turn around. The gun rammed harder against her skull.

"Oh, I don't think so, sweetheart." Ward's hand reached around, and he snatched the knife out of her hand. "See, I trusted you once, and you shot me full of drugs."

Still reeling from the fact he got the jump on her, she calculated the number of weapons she still had within grabbing range. She could take him. She had before.

The thought almost made her smile, but she went with a shrug instead. "A misunderstanding."

"Then you won't mind if I use that trick on you this time."

That couldn't happen. She had to stay on her feet to neutralize Tigana. "A woman has to be careful. Some men are nasty on dates."

A deep male chuckle then… "She's got you there."

The sound of a second male voice screeched across her senses. One she could handle without trouble. Two put her at a disadvantage. If number two was anything like Ward, he was bigger and heavier than her. Then there was the issue of Ward's anger. She couldn't gauge how out of control that was at this point.

She blew out a long breath as a list of possible attack strategies filled her head. "You brought a friend. Fantastic."

The pressure against her head eased, and before she could blink, two men stood in front of her. Ward's shoulders blocked most of her view into the woods beyond, but she recognized the other one. Brown hair and green eyes, good looking in that would-likely-break-your-heart kind of way.

He'd attracted a lot of attention back at the resort with his supposed businessman-looking-for-an-island invest-ment front. Had an unusual name…she pulled it out of her mind somewhere. Ford. This guy and Ward looked like a matched set, all tall and dangerous with a smooth-talking calm about them.

And liars. Not businessmen. No doubt about it. The only mystery was why it took her so long to see it.

Ward motioned toward his friend with the big gun and even bigger frown. "This is Ford."

"If you try to stick a needle in me, I'll break your arm," Ford said.

Well, there was no confusing that statement. She appreciated that. "He's charming."

Ford nodded. "I thought we should understand each other from the beginning."

Her gaze kept zipping back to Ward. She hated the energy that bounced between her and him even more. She'd spent her entire career dealing with controlling assholes and assholes who thought having a penis put them in charge. But there was something different about Ward. When he looked at her, she knew she had his full attention. His gaze didn't wander. His eyes stayed even and clear.

"How did you sneak up on me?" She had to know. She'd scouted every inch of the area from above. She'd been trained to pick up sounds and see clues others missed. Yet these two, each one pushing over six feet, walked right up without tipping her off. Really, it was embarrassing.

Ward smiled. "Trade secret."

That sounded like an admission to her. Of what, was the question. "Which trade is that again?"

"Watch her." Ward handed his gun to Ford then started patting her down.

"Is this necessary?" And why didn't his hands on her bother her one bit?

Ward dropped one of her knives to the ground and then another before holding up the last one. "Apparently."

"Where's the needle?" Ford asked.

"I only had two." Which ticked her off. If she'd known she'd have to beat back a bunch of guys pretending to be office types, she would have brought vials of the knock-out drug.

"Huh." Ford shrugged. "That's a shame."

"Says the guy who didn't get stuck with it," Ward grumbled as he slid his fingers into her boot and took out the small gun she'd stashed there.

This wasn't good. He'd been thorough, and everything she brought with her except for a small thin blade taped to her hip now lay on the ground. That made escape tough. She thought about kicking Ward in the head and running, but Ford looked ready and willing to shoot.

Her life would be much easier if the Americans would have just stayed in America. The least they could do was admit who they were...and then it hit her. The mirrored stances, the weapons, the we-like-to-kill attitudes. They were professionals. Not guns-for-hire or weekend warriors. They played the same game she played.

The pieces clicked into place. It would make sense for the United States to have people on the ground looking after Tigana. Those covert tracking skills and Ward's carefully crafted cover. And they had that look, which would mean neutralizing them and shooing them away before they trashed her assignment.

"You're CIA." She didn't ask because she suddenly didn't need to.

Ward glanced up right before he stretched to his feet. "What are you?"

She noticed Ward didn't bother to deny the accusation. Didn't confirm it either. "A woman working on an island."

Ford shifted his legs and adjusted his battle stance. "That's annoying."

"Tell me about it," Ward said. "You have one more chance here, Tasha."

"Or?" No way would they drag out the interrogation tactics. If they tried, she would go out screaming.

"Spill it, or we tie you to a tree and leave you out here." Ward clapped his hand against the bark right near her head, probably to reinforce his point.

She didn't need the highlight. She understood. Got it and now called up her bored tone to telegraph her lack of concern back to him. "Oh, please."

"Try me." But, really, the tying up thing didn't sound like a great option. Less painful than other options but hugely problematic. They weren't the only ones around here with a cover to protect, and Tigana's men could come back at any time.

"You did knock him out twice." Ford winced. Even made an annoying hissing sound. "For future reference, men don't like that sort of thing."

She backed up a step, small and hopefully not noticeable. With them crowding in, she needed her back covered and a bit of leverage. Wedging her body against the tree provided both. "I have a job to do."

"Uh-huh…which is?" Ward had the nerve to twirl her knife.

Twirl. It.

Her heel hit a tree root and she rocked her weight to keep from showing any real movement. "You two are in my way."

This time Ward winked at her. "Right back at ya, sweetheart."

"Stop with the endearments." She'd found him much more attractive back when he sipped drinks at the bar. Armed and grumbling Ward annoyed her. Unfortunately, the attractive part didn't go away.

Ward glanced down toward her shoes. "And you should stop fidgeting since you're not the one with the weapons."

Damn it. "It's a bit uncomfortable standing here with you two staring at me in angry-male mode and pretending to be threatening."

"Pretending?" Ford asked in a low voice that didn't pretend at all.

"I'm betting you can handle yourself just fine." Ward tapped his shoulder, right by the second injection site. "I've felt your handiwork with needles."

"Do you two need some alone time?" Ford asked.

She could handle one of them, but the smartass overload from Ford was a bit much. She stopped glaring at him and faced Ward again. "Why did you bring him?"

"He usually has cash for beer." Ward shot Ford a quick glance. "That sort of thing comes in handy."

She didn't know whether to be impressed with Ward's ability to joke or to be ticked off. The whole thing where he simultaneously scoped out the area while keeping just out of kicking range from her looked familiar. She'd been trained. He'd been trained. It made for difficult escape planning.

But it was time to inch them toward some sort of resolution that didn't include one or more of their bodies scattered on the ground. "Do you need that beer when you're out here chasing down bad guys?"

Ward stilled. "Who do you think I'm chasing?"

She judged the distance between them one last time. She could lunge, and Ford would likely shoot her. Not a helpful solution. Still not an option, which was a damn shame.

That left the new and even riskier tactic of compromise. She could work with them...or pretend to. She didn't intend to tangle with other agents or share the credit with another country, but she doubted these two would skulk back to Langley quietly. At the very least, she could use their resources and the strength their double team provided. That meant confirming her position as an ally. A reluctant one, but still an ally.

She looked from Ward to Ford and back again. Her gut told her to connect with Ward, though she feared some body parts other than her gut were guiding her decision. "Maybe there's a man here, on this island, who shouldn't be."

Silence whipped through the wooded area. Even the leaves seemed to stop rustling as she held her breath and waited to see what Ward would do.

After a few more seconds he nodded. "That might be true."

Looks like they were definitely playing the same game. It was the only thing that stopped her from grabbing the tree trunk, spinning around, and nailing Ward in the chest with a roundhouse kick. "Maybe this man needs to be taken out before he destabilizes Fiji."

Ward stopped flipping her knife around. "Or starts playing with all the toys he brought here with him."

"Yeah, maybe." Those were the first words Ford said on the topic.

With that, some of the tightness across her shoulders eased and the ticking at the base of her neck stopped. "Are you two ready to confirm you're CIA?"

Ford swore under his breath as she stared at Ward. "Apparently you suck at this work. She clearly made you before now."

Ward didn't even spare his partner a glance. "Don't make me sorry I brought you along."

The intensity of Ward's focus made something in her stomach clench, and not in an angry way. She didn't trust him and didn't particularly like him. That whole charming act wore thin fast, or that's what she told herself. But they could forge a silent agreement of sorts. One that meant she couldn't kick, punch, or shoot anyone up with drugs. Good thing she had other skills.

She answered Ford's question even though it really wasn't directed at her. "I saw Ward looking through my bag before we left the bar for my place last night."

He'd palmed her wallet. Later he'd diverted her attention and done a quick bag check. Subtle but effective. Just not quite effective enough.

Ford shot Ward the side eye. "Sounds like someone needs a refresher course in subterfuge."

"I almost missed the bag check, but combine the behavior with the fact it's pretty clear he's not on the island for the buffet, and I got suspicious." Then a bit frustrated that a night with Ward couldn't happen.

"Who the hell are you?" Ford asked.

"You really haven't figured it out?" she asked, not bothering to cover what to them would be an accent.

Ward shook his head. "British Intelligence."

"MI6?" Ford's eyes widened. "Get the fuck out."

"Makes sense." The shock started to leave Ward's voice.

Ford's frown suggested he was having trouble believing. "Does it?"

If they kept talking to each other they wouldn't need her for this conversation. Now there was a tempting thought.

"We'll get confirmation." The amusement left Ford's face, and he went back to scowling. "How exactly?" She doubted MI6 opened its files whenever the CIA called. Especially not in this case, where she wasn't even supposed to be in this country and neither were they.

When he ignored the question, she leaned against the tree, this time not for leverage. From the cramped quarters in the tree, her right thigh muscle kept twitching. Taking some weight off it helped.

Ward tucked her gun into the back waistband of his pants. "That's a bit much, isn't it?"

Since they both stared at her, she wondered if she'd missed part of the discussion. "What?"

"Your name is Natasha and you're a spy?" Ward scoffed. "I mean, come on."

Really, that was his concern? Man, these Langley boys misfired sometimes. "Were you this big of a pain in the ass back at the resort?"

"No," Ward said.

Ford nodded. "Absolutely."

Maybe she didn't need them after all. They got easily sidetracked. Even now they stood close enough to striking range that they should be on high alert. Instead, they joked and slouched. Not exactly prime examples of the CIA type...not that she'd liked all that many of the ones she'd met.

"Now that we've had our introductions, you both need to leave." She tried to sound calm about it since some men got all defensive if a woman showed her strength. And if one of them called her a bitch, she'd put him in a headlock with her thighs.

Ward didn't move, but the air around him did. It was as if something inside him snapped to attention. "Not happening."

"You're going to blow *my* op." She looked over at Ford. "Lose the gun."

"She's bossy." Ford smiled as if he seemed happy at the idea.

Time for a little tough love or a reality check—whatever they called it. "You guys trained Tigana. He went to college in your country. Harvard, right?" Before Ward could answer, she plowed ahead. "He enjoyed the funding you sent his way and the Stinger missiles you provided for him to shoot down planes and flip over armored vehicles."

"That clearly was a miscalculation," Ford mumbled under his breath.

Ward held up a hand. "What my friend means is the US had no involvement with any weapons this hypothetical piece of shit may or may not have."

There was no need for confirmation, but she had it now. "He destroyed his own country. Now he has his eye on Fiji as a new playground, and you guys are here because you need to clean up your mess."

Ward shrugged. "Admittedly, he is not the finest example of the US education system."

Not exactly the response she expected. "He's going to start a military coup, shake up the Pacific, then move on from there with his cache of surface-to-air missiles. I can't let any of that happen."

And this guy would do it. He grabbed or bought—that part of the intel wasn't clear—weapons that were easy to carry and invented to inflict maximum damage from a distance. The technical term was MANPADS, Man-Portable Air-Defense System. It could shoot three miles and depended on infrared homing, which meant a shooter could fire then run. No need to wait around for targeting. Which also meant Tigana qualified as a very dangerous and armed man at the moment.

"Uh-huh, yeah." Ward repeated the phrase several times as she talked. "That's an impressive speech, but this dictator is the US's problem and we're here to handle him."

There it was. That American can-do attitude.

She was not a fan. "Just the two of you?"

"Not to be too obvious, but I would point out you're also alone." Ford motioned to the area around them.

And since they both kept checking the woods, scanning and assessing, they knew she stood by herself until they bumbled along. "Am I?"

"I'm starting to understand what you see in her," Ford said.

Ward ignored the comment and never broke eye contact with her. "Where's your partner?"

She'd already played the overshare game. Disclosing would lead to more questions. Her debrief after this op would take months at this rate. "I'm done talking."

"I'd hate to be out there and shoot your partner by accident." Ford held up his gun.

As if she forgot he had the damn thing. It was the number one deterrent from doing something closer to dumb than brave on the fighting scale. "Missing."

Ward leaned in as if trying to hear her. "Excuse me?"

Okay, this last piece they could know because she just might need their help with an extraction. "Gareth went radio silent. Last I knew he was scouting out an area about three kilometers from here."

Ward frowned. "Gareth?"

"Kilometers?" Ford made a face that suggested he was trying to calculate something in his head. "I hate math."

She could probably find better sidekicks if she closed her eyes and pointed. "Why don't you two head back to the resort and—"

"We'll break up. I'll take the Brit and go east. You head west. Radio silence. We'll use the clicks rather than talking

to cover our respective positions. I'll have you on GPS."
It was as if Ward flipped a switch and entered leadership mode. Gone was the fun-loving guy on vacation. He barked orders like a battlefield commander.

Good. It gave her hope he might not accidentally trip over a tree root and shoot her.

"You sure it's a good idea that you double up with Tasha?" Ford smacked Ward on the shoulder. "After all, she did kick your ass twice already."

"He grabbed all of my weapons." She thought she'd point that out since she planned to demand them all back before they took off on the suggested trek.

"Right, because you need a weapon to cause trouble." Ward shot her a look that said he'd learned his lesson. "I doubt that."

She didn't hate being seen from a position of strength. She could use that later, when she grabbed Tigana and left the CIA boys behind. "I'll take that as a compliment."

"I used to like British people…" Ford's comment just hung out there.

"No worries," Ward said. "She doesn't have a choice but to play nice."

Not true, but if he thought so she had an advantage. But…"How do you figure that?"

Ward took a step toward her. Got in nice and close. "I'll burn your cover if you so much as nod your head in a way I don't like."

She wanted to shove against his chest or grab her knife back. Instead she stood there. Something in his tone and the intense heat she saw in his eyes hypnotized her.

Right before her common sense took a final nosedive, she landed one more verbal shot. "You'll blow your own at the same time, genius."

"You act as if Ford and I are the only two people on this assignment for the US." Ward's eyebrow lifted. "Wrong."

Looked like underneath all the games and jokes there lurked a guy who liked to play chicken. Interesting. But this was not her first day on the job. She was career MI6 and had spanked CIA guys older than Ward on jobs when they got in the way. "It's a small island. I'd know if there were more of you."

"You willing to take that chance? To possibly let Tigana slip away?" Ward asked in an even, emotionless tone.

The guy had developed a poker face all of a sudden. His blank expression didn't give anything away. *Good trick.*

It was an impressive bait-and-switch. She'd been sold one version of Ward. Now she faced down another. Commanding, a guy fully in charge and trained as a weapon.

He just got hotter, which sucked for her.

"He has to go down," she said referring to Tigana, though it applied to all the men she knew on the island at this moment.

Ward nodded. "Then we'll do it together."

"Aw, how sweet."

Yeah, the likelihood of her shooting Ford grew with each passing second when he said things like that. But she kept her attention on Ward. She hadn't seen it before, but it was clear now: he was the one she had to go through to get anything done.

He just needed to realize she was in charge, so she acted like it. "For the next two hours, we're on the same side. We check the area, gather intel, then meet back at my room at the resort. We need to know how many men Tigana has, the structures, the resources. And I'll look for Gareth."

Ford elbowed Ward. "She thinks she's the boss."

She answered that. "She is."

"You forget we have the guns." Ward held his weapon up again, just inside her line of vision.

She wasn't any more impressed this time than the last. "It's cute you think that means something to me."

Ward's lip twitched. "Then lead the way, boss."

Chapter Four

AFTER BREAKING OFF from Ford as planned, Ward and Tasha walked in silence for fifteen minutes. Ward kept track of her, the weapons, and the area around him. Even now, a gun touched his back, one rested against his palm, and another thudded against his leg in his pocket as he walked.

Ford had given the prearranged radio signal confirming her cover checked out. Getting the intel so fast meant someone in the United States or the United Kingdom—or both—played hardball or called in favors. Both countries likely denied being in Fiji. Ward didn't want to know what Ford said or what threats passed back and forth to get the information on Tasha. Well, he did, but he could wait until after they grabbed the Stinger missiles away from Tigana.

But Ward wasn't sharing anything he'd learned from Ford's simple coded message with Tasha right now. No, the next move belonged to her. Ward vowed to stay quiet, even if it meant he had to chew through his tongue to bite back some smartass comment or worse, keep from making an unfortunate and untimely pass at her.

With each step, they tunneled deeper into the greenery. Humidity slapped his face. The grouping of trees grew thicker until the leaves had to be swatted away. The whole time, Ward waited for Tasha to unload, yell, issue orders—something.

In minute sixteen, she broke.

"If we find Tigana, I'll decide what we do next." She pushed a branch to the side as she forged a trail where none existed.

There it was. "You've made it clear you think you're in charge."

"I know that tone and your type." She shot him a sideways glance that telegraphed *you're an asshole* without actually saying it. "Don't pretend we're agreeing with each other."

He watched his footing, careful to make as little noise as possible as he placed each step. Not easy to do when a guy weighed one-eighty, but Ward had honed this skill. He could sneak in and attack without warning.

"Is it just me, or do you have a problem with Americans in general?" he asked.

"Your country is fine. It's your intelligence service that needs some work."

Ward said the same thing at least ten times per day, only not in those words because they had a stick-up-her-ass ring to them. Sending two men to take out a crazed dictator with big guns amounted to a CIA suicide mission. Yet here he was, in the middle of a makeshift jungle, sporting limited weapons and partnering with a pissed-off Brit with a needle-poking habit.

Maybe he really should have gone into finance.

"I'm not necessarily disagreeing, but what mission are you referring to exactly that the CIA screwed up?" The woman sounded as if she spoke from experience, and that had him listening. "Maybe if I knew where your anger came from—"

She stopped and stared at him. "I hate men who think all strong women are angry."

Well, that explained the thin lips and eyes spitting with fire. The woman clearly thought he was an ass. Not something that normally bothered him, but on this subject matter, it pissed him off.

They didn't have time, but he stepped in closer and took a few seconds anyway. "I called you angry because you threatened to rip my balls off earlier today, not because I use anger as a code word for *bitchy* or some other sexist nonsense."

She hesitated for a second as her gaze scanned his face; then she nodded. "Understood."

That went easier than he expected. He didn't question the stroke of good luck. "Now that we have that settled, tell me your issue with the US intelligence community."

"Let's just say I've had trouble in the past with the CIA getting into the middle of my operations and screwing them up." Then she took off again, slicing her hand through the heavy vegetation and moving at a speed that should have had her tripping but didn't.

The whole take-no-prisoners attitude…so fucking hot.

He waited until he drew up next to her again to dive back into the conversation. "Sounds as if you were dealing with amateurs."

"But you think you're different, I assume." Her voice no longer vibrated with fury, and the corners of her mouth twitched as if she fought off a smile.

"I don't know those guys—they were guys, right?" When she nodded he joined her. "Yeah, figured."

He knew the type—blowhard, in control, my-way-or-I'll-shoot-you types. A few lingered the halls of the agency, vying for attention and recognition. They tended to lack longevity. Anyone worth anything in the field blended in. A healthy ego was mandatory. A need to be noticed got people killed, and he'd seen more than one innocent caught in the crossfire.

"Don't write off the entire agency based on a few CIA assholes." He doubted she gave much thought to any of the losers she passed on the way up her career ladder, but he felt the need to say it anyway.

This time she did smile. "Are you trying to charm me?"

That face. *Damn.* "Would it work?"

"No." But her tone suggested otherwise.

He forced thoughts of her naked and under him out of his head and concentrated on making his point… once he remembered what it was. If he planned on putting his life in her hands, and it might come to that, she needed to know he did not screw around when it came to the job.

Thinking that building a bit of trust might not be a bad thing, he handed her one of her knives—one he could wrestle away from her without trouble if this turned out to be a miscalculation. "Here. Just don't use it on me."

She stared at it, then at him. "Look at you acting against type."

He decided to ignore the shot. "My point is I don't know which agents you're talking about. But if you're asking if I'm dependable and focused despite the flirting, yes."

Her smiled only brightened. "You sound a bit like one of the Queen's corgis."

"That's a dog, right?" Not exactly a compliment. He wasn't sure what the hell to do with the comment.

"And about the flirting..."

She'd called him a dog, so this really didn't have anywhere to go but up. At least he hoped that was true. "Yes?"

"Do you have any limits?"

His mind blanked. He'd been listening to her, watching her, all while keeping his senses locked on alert for distinct sounds and the approach of anything he'd need to shoot, strangle, or cut down. Now he knew he'd missed something. "I don't know what you're asking."

"I'm assuming the flirting was part of some grand plan to lure me into bed and once there, ask me questions about what I've seen happening on the island."

Whack.

Another branch took a hit, this time with the help of her knife. Ward started thinking she might be visualizing his head as she took each swing.

He went with a quick-and-dirty answer in the hope she wouldn't turn the knife on him. "Nope."

"You were pretending to be on holiday—"

"Holiday?" The word dragged his attention away from her lean arm muscles and the expertise with which she cut those branches. One long arc and she created an opening in front of her that they both could slip through. *So damn hot.*

She shrugged. "I believe you call it a *vacation*."

Looked like they had a language barrier of sorts after all. "Ah, right. Go ahead."

"You're saying you weren't trying to lure me into bed with all that smooth talk back at the bar?" She wasn't looking at him now. The steady rhythm of cutting and holding back her steps for a fraction of a second as each branch fell guided their way.

"Oh, I was." He waited until she glanced at him because he wanted eye contact. "But that wasn't for the job. It was all for me."

Her arm dropped to her side, and she stood frozen. "Huh."

The relative quiet gave way to something. A slight swish. A rumble, low but clear.

They had company.

"Hold up." He put a hand on her arm and drew her body even with his. With his head bowed he whispered in her ear. Felt her shiver. "Wait."

"You hear something?" Her tone dropped to match his. They spoke at a level that barely registered as a whisper.

"Maybe." He wasn't sure if he said the word out loud or just nodded.

The rumble grew louder. Ward concentrated, focusing in on the sound that didn't match the others. Blocked out the wind and the rustle of branches. Ignored the dull thwap from where she tapped the side of the knife against her leg.

Through his training he'd learned how to survive and how to kill. But this, the ability to pick out sounds and magnify them in his head, came to him as a kid. Years of practice and focus brought him to this point. He'd endured hours of study at the Farm with agency instructors investigating the skill in the hope of teaching it to others but failing.

Ward chalked his strange gift up to his upbringing. In a household where no one talked and everyone obeyed his father's word without question, Ward had learned to thrive in silence. And it served him well now.

"Where—" Tasha's words cut off when Ward squeezed her arm. "Right."

"Men." He knew by the way the footsteps fell. The heaviness said male, and the echo grew louder. "Fifty feet and closing."

She glanced over his shoulder, but Ward knew she wouldn't see anything. Not through the thick brush and blanket of branches. The potential attackers didn't speak, and picking up their exact location and direction proved difficult. But Ward knew. They had seconds only before the group—he thought no more than three and possibly only two—moved into view.

As soon as he saw the attackers, the attackers would see him. With that advantage gone, the shooting would begin. Bullets and noise, and Ward knew they'd be outnumbered. So, he had to get the jump now.

Raw energy thrummed off Tasha. She hadn't moved, but the air around her changed, as if charged with electricity. "We should go."

"Too late." In a few quick moves, Ward had a gun tucked behind Tasha's back and one in his least favorite place for a weapon, the front of his pants. A knife sat in his pocket within easy grabbing and throwing range. That weapon would be his last defense. If he reached for that one, he'd likely do it on the way down.

"What are you—" Her gaze flew up to meet his.

He knew the second she picked up the shuffling sound. Emotion drained from her face, and her eyes met his. Something subtle in the way she moved and the stiffness across her shoulders suggested she'd flipped into battle mode.

He nodded, trying to telegraph the need for her to play along and, if necessary, shoot around him while using his body as a shield. He needed to believe she handled a gun half as well as she did a needle full of that junk to knock him out.

"Don't fight me." That was all he got out before he put the only realistic plan into motion.

An iguana scurried into the brush as Ward pushed her back deeper into the tree. Footsteps thundered around them, and he lowered his head. His mouth covered hers right before something crunched behind him. He tried to concentrate on the sounds of the forest area and the incoming attack party, but her mouth had his attention zapping.

Her lips were soft, and the kiss hot. He strained to listen, to keep his mind on the job, but the kiss sucked him under. She tasted as good as he suspected she would. Her fingers slipped into his hair, and her body brushed against his.

Lips touching with his hands on her hips. He kissed her once, faster than he wanted, giving into the need that had been building in his gut since the first time he met her.

Blinding heat rocked through him, then he wrestled his control back. They could not do this. Not here. Not with the audience he felt watching them through the trees.

"Hey." A male voice, sharp and demanding.

Ward broke away from her. Ignored her swollen lips and the clenching of her fingers into his biceps as he glanced over his shoulder, playing every inch of the interrupted angry boyfriend.

"This is private…" Ward saw the two men step into the small clearing Tasha's tree hacking had created. His gaze went to their assault weapons and then back to the men trying to sneak a peek at Tasha from behind him. Fury rushed over him, but he hid it under an act of wide-eyed surprise. "Oh, wait…what…"

The taller of the two gestured with a lift of his chin. "What are you doing out here?"

Like a well-timed machine and without a word of direction, Tasha slipped the gun out of his waistband. Ward felt it brush against his skin; then it was gone. Now he could turn around without either getting shot or having to draw. There was still hope to diffuse this situation without bloodshed.

He did just that. With hands raised and wearing the frown of a tourist confused by having weapons flashing for him to see, he slowly turned to face the two unwanted visitors head-on. "Exactly what it looks like. I'm spending some time with my girl."

The shorter man stared at Tasha. Without a signal from his brain, Ward moved to shield her. If the way she knocked him out earlier were any indication, she could handle this situation. But that didn't mean he liked some asswipe dressed as a bought-and-paid-for soldier of convenience gawking at her.

"You're in a restricted area," the taller one said. He kept his finger off the trigger, but it was right there.

Tasha slid the gun into the back waistband of Ward's pants, then her hands went to his shoulders as she peeked at the men in front of her. "We're on a hike."

The slight vibration in her voice. The subtle rearming. Ward had to give her credit. She played it smooth and genuine right down to the intimacy she wove around them as a pretend couple.

"Keep going." The tall one kept up the nodding. This time he gestured inland and away from the direction of Tigana's believed hideout. "That way."

Ward wrapped an arm around his back to touch the small of hers. He aimed for a loving gesture, but his focus stayed on the weapons—theirs and his. He wanted the guns he and Tasha held hidden and unseen. That required shuffling but innocent tourists would shuffle and panic and possibly even beg.

Ward was about to try a few of those options when the smaller guy moved. Didn't say a word, but that finger inched closer to the trigger.

"Wait," the smaller one said. He stepped right in front of Ward, which sent Tasha crashing against his back. "How did you get here?"

"Hike." Ward kept it short, just as he'd been trained to do. Too many details signaled lies. Too much information made it easy to get wrapped up and babbling. And Ward was not a babbler.

The taller one now stood next to his partner. They both stared, and neither showed any signs of backing down, which was a shame. Ward had hoped not to kill anyone today.

"Where are you parked?" the taller one asked.

"About two miles that way." Ward pointed but had no idea how accurate the gesture came off. He hadn't measured, but the distance didn't matter. At this rate, at least two of them would not be standing by the time the discussion ended.

The taller one maintained eye contact with Tasha. "A truck?"

"No," she answered back in an equally clipped tone.

Energy pulsed off her. Ward stood there, taking it in, feeling her body rev up even though she showed no signs of even sweating.

The shorter one reached around Ward and grabbed her arm. The touch had Ward's senses firing and rage burning his brain from the inside out. He shoved the man away. "What do you think you're doing?"

The men looked at each other before the taller one started speaking again. "You need to come with us."

"We'll head back to the resort and—" This time the guy yanked and Tasha stumbled. Ward guessed the pseudofall had some strategic purpose he couldn't see behind his back. Not that the intent mattered. He took mental inventory of the weapons on him and picked the one guaranteed to inflict maximum damage on this guy. "Do not touch her."

With that the men moved back. Gone was any casual discussion. The air took on a suffocating thickness. The guns no longer hung in front of the men. Now the barrels pointed at the dead center of Ward's chest. He didn't love the change.

"Step away from the woman." The shorter one barked out orders as if he thought they'd strike fear.

Not even close.

"I don't think so." Ward's arm inched farther back along the side of his leg and closer to the gun stored behind him.

Tasha's fingers tightened against his skin. "It's okay, honey."

Ward barely heard her. The sensation of her pulling the gun away from his body filled his brain. "You sure?"

She clearly had a plan; it involved bullets, and Ward wished he knew the rest. He'd have to make a solid guess based on what he knew—this woman would attack without remorse. He respected that.

"We'll be fine."

That voice. The brush of her hair against his cheek. The woman did know how to soothe. Ward hoped her shot proved half as good, because his choices carried some limitations. Thank goodness for the knife within reach.

The taps came next. Her fingers drummed a steady beat on his back. Her body barely moved. This woman had some practice hiding her movements.

Ward's admiration grew as his mind clicked into gear. They had one shot at this. Take out both guys with minimum noise. That was the plan…well, it was *his* plan.

The tapping pattern clicked down from five. When she reached one, he hit the ground. Dropping to a crouch, he let his knife fly as her hand rose. The blade flipped through the air and landed in the taller guy's shoulder. He let out a squeal as his shooting arm dropped to his side.

Ward didn't wait. He crashed into the guy before he could raise the gun again. The forest erupted with noise as their feet trampled the fallen leaves and the tall one hit the ground on his back. Ward pulled out the blade and was on him in less than a second. With the handle of the knife between his teeth, Ward grabbed the man's head and smashed it against the ground. Once, twice, then his eyes rolled back in his head and his body turned limp.

Grunts sounded behind him, and Ward spun around, ready for the next fight. Tasha was already locked in battle with the smaller guy. Her kick smacked into the guy's chest just as Ward scrambled to his feet. Off balance, the guy fumbled for his gun and started yelling. The sound cut off when Ward wrapped an arm around the guy's neck—put it right in the crook of his elbow—and squeezed. Three seconds, and the guy crumpled into a heap next to his friend.

A cursory check of pockets revealed a decided lack of identifying information. No surprise there. If these two were mercenaries—they certainly had some training, just not enough—they knew not to possess anything that could trace back to actual names.

Ward grabbed a radio off the small guy and an extra gun. He handed the latter to Tasha. If he had more than one, so should she.

"Nice kick." By a very impressive leg. That was the type of agility he could admire and did. That and her ability to fight without so much as breathing hard.

Everything this woman did was hot.

After a quick check, she took the weapon and slipped it into her pocket. "So, I can see that you do fight when you have to."

"Did you have any doubts?"

She didn't hesitate. "Yes."

Well, that was annoying. "I'm going to see this as a glass-half-full situation."

"How so?"

"In your eyes I don't have anywhere to go but up." He tried to keep the words light, but the sentiment behind them was all too real. He'd never had anyone doubt his judgment or abilities before and he didn't like it now.

But on one level they did understand each other. After that kiss, maybe more than one. They worked the same way.

"Is your head okay?" she asked out of nowhere. "I need to know you can handle this."

"Despite your efforts, I'm fine. Hurts like hell, but I'll live."

She frowned. "I guess that's good."

Without checking with each other, they started securing the scene. Each one took a man and conducted a final search of pockets and the area. The next step would be hiding the bodies and covering tracks. If they couldn't come up with a solid plan, they'd have to move from quieting the mercenaries to killing them. Ward didn't relish that.

A year ago he witnessed a bloodbath on the job. Stood there as armed gunmen emptied out a refugee camp. The dirt ran with blood by the time the gunfire stopped. Bodies piled upon bodies. Women and children thrown around like garbage. Ward took a vow of humanity that day. Sticking to it challenged him every fucking day on the job.

So many orders. So much death. Years of working with one side in some country only to take an abrupt turn and undermine the very people he'd helped put in power a few years later. It was a stupid, endless, and necessary game. He just grew weary of playing.

Tigana was just one example. Having seen the file with the information about the torture he inflicted on his own people, Ward knew the man needed to be terminated, no matter what the mission objectives were. That didn't mean they had to leave a trail of bodies across Fiji. The lower the loss of life, the better this would be.

"These two are going to wake up," Tasha said as she stepped between the bodies.

"Lucky for you I brought some of these and gags." Ward pulled a wad of zip ties out of his lower pants pocket. "Yours, I believe."

She fingered the plastic strips in his palm. "We're not killing them?"

"Do we need to?" He tensed as he waited for her response.

She held up a tie. "You're the one who said any idiot can break those."

"Not the way I use them."

She smiled. "I'll remember that."

Chapter Five

FIFTEEN MINUTES LATER, they dragged the bodies into the heavy greenery and Ward started covering the marks left in the dirt. Tasha watched, trying to shake off the prickling sensation at the back of her neck.

On any other day, any other job, the mission objectives would trump and they'd eliminate potential witnesses. She didn't see a reason to stray from that now. These two would wake up and cause trouble that far outweighed the potential of their bodies being found or what the combination of heat and animals would do to the corpses.

She stood there with the unused zip ties hanging from her fingers. "We have a problem."

"I can come up with six without even thinking about it very hard." Without so much as breaking a sweat, Ward covered every footstep. Removed any sign humans once waited there.

Impressive work but not good enough. The stakes were too high. "We can't leave them alive."

He nodded but didn't take out his gun or do anything to suggest he agreed. "We need to watch the area from a distance so we can track movements in and out, count guards. Those sorts of things."

She agreed with the plans and highlighted one of the "to do" items on the list. "We have to relocate."

"You mean move?"

She wasn't in the mood for a word debate. "I have a car. We need to pick it up on the way out."

"Car as in the truck?" He shook his head. "If so, it sounds like they found it, which means they know what it looks like, and wherever we take it we'll be tracked. Hell, with the number of people on this island, they could already know it's yours."

He assumed she would be dumb enough to use her own vehicle on this job. Typical. The guy needed a little work on his how-to-play-nice-with-others skills. "Wrong. Tasha the bartender hasn't done anything wrong and doesn't drive an SUV."

"So, there's nothing in that vehicle that will get your ass arrested or shot?" He leaned in closer. "If you're as competent as I think you are, you've got weapons stored in there."

That show of faith in her skills sounded better. Not great, but better than some of the men she got paired with. "My bum is fine."

He frowned. "What?"

The man got thrown off by simple words. Lethal and stumbling for a British dictionary. For some reason, that combination when mixed with the lean body and escape skills snagged her interest. "The weapons are locked down."

"They will take a blowtorch to the truck, and you know it." Ward pointed to the lifeless bodies next to her feet. "These two are trained mercenaries. They were the scouting party. Can you imagine the skills on the experienced men in the group?"

Not a bad argument. She was willing to listen to more but held on to her veto. "So, what's the plan?"

After a quick check of the direction from which the two armed men came, Ward stood in front of her again. "Secure and hide the bodies as fast as we can, double back to take a look at the truck from an elevated, safe distance, and then once we know who is where and how many we have to shoot through, we hunt down Tigana."

He'd clearly given the afternoon agenda some thought. She appreciated his planning. "Sounds like you've done this before."

"Since the last part of the plan is to run like hell if they see us, you can assume that I'm a professional. Unless you think that's an amateur move—then forget I said it."

Oh my God, that smile. He aimed it at her, and her control puddled at her feet. She didn't lose sight of her job, but she did entertain the idea of running her hands all over him if they ever finished this assignment and got to a safe place. "We have to move in on Tigana."

"We have to live through the next few hours first."

"You know how to kill the mood." But those priorities made sense. They also reinforced her belief that they needed a more permanent solution for the men at her feet.

He leveled a serious flat-lipped stare in her direction. "Let's hope that's the last time you think that about me."

"We're not having sex." The words shot out before she could stop them.

"Well, not here." He glanced around the hard ground. "That would be stupid."

"Not ever." She tried to signal her brain to shut up, but the words kept dribbling out. Last thing she needed was for him to know *she* was thinking about sex.

She shifted her weight, and her foot hit against something. Before she could glance down, a hand clamped around her ankle. One hard yank, and her knee buckled. On the way down she reached for the gun Ward gave her, jerking at her clothes to free it and fire.

The shot stopped her. It rang out, echoing through the rough terrain. The grip on her loosened right as Ward grabbed her around the waist. She picked up the telltale metallic smell she'd been trained to detect and saw Ward's weapon on the way back down to his side.

She leaned into Ward for an extra second, more out of shock from being caught off guard by the gunman than anything else. People rarely got the jump on her.

That would teach her to think about sex on the job.

She stood up straight and tugged on the bottom of her T-shirt. Retucked it into her shorts. At least she'd changed from yesterday's outfit before heading out to find Tigana. In this humidity clothes stayed bearable for only so long.

"I got the impression you were going for minimal loss of life here," she said as she stared at the two bodies, one lifeless and the other unmoving.

"No one touches you." Ward's eyes burned with a new intensity.

It sounded like a vow, and she took it as one. Too stunned to say anything else, she went with the first lame thing that popped into her head. "Okay."

When the second guy stirred at her feet, she didn't hesitate. Gun out and barrel down, she fired. The man's face fell back to the ground with a thud.

Ward winced but otherwise did not move at her impromptu shot. He looked down at the man with the blood now pooling around his head.

Ward stepped back and out of blood range. "Was that necessary?"

No way was she justifying saving them both from a shootout. Still… "We both know he'd have somehow gotten free and blown our cover, and that's if he didn't kill you first."

Ward nodded. "Now he won't be doing anything."

A cryptic comment. One she jumped right over. "Right."

"You're in charge." He let out a long breath. "So, lead."

She almost felt bad about what she was going to say. "I'm happy you remembered that."

If anything his frown deepened. "Why?"

"You need to start digging." She skimmed the tip of her boot over the ground and listened to pebbles scrape against the sole. "We need these guys buried, and you should hurry."

AN HOUR LATER Ward's muscles still burned. Digging in dirt filled with roots will do that to a guy. Without a shovel he had to use her knife to pound at the ground. When she'd joined in, the task went faster but not by much. They'd removed enough soil, rocks, and fallen leaves to put the bodies at only a slightly higher level than the rest of the forest floor. Moving boulders and branches did the rest to provide cover.

Now they lay next to each other on their stomachs, flat against the ground and hiding behind low bushes on a small hill a football field's length away from the SUV, which he could only see with binoculars. Good thing she carried a pair with her.

More strategy on her part. Like how she'd picked a cleared area to park but that the forest walls covered on three sides. That made spotting the gunmen easy. With their vantage point above, there was nowhere for the men to hide.

She took the binoculars out of his hands and took a long look, scanning the entire range. Her gaze moved, then stopped and doubled back.

"Well, that's going to be a problem." She handed him the binoculars and pointed. "Look about fifty meters to the left."

"Any chance you could talk in feet?"

"No." She dropped her head between her arms. "You're right. They're going to tear it apart."

He'd just spotted two more guys approaching with the tools. Looked like a sledgehammer and some sort of bolt cutters. Anything could be in the large bag the one guy had slung over his shoulder.

Yeah, all trouble, but her comment caught his attention. He glanced over at her. "Say that again."

She lifted her head. "Can't you see—"

"The part where I'm right." Out of all the mindless talking and all those nights of flirting at the resort, that sentence stood out.

She ripped the binoculars out of his hands again. "Gloating is unattractive."

Tucking the compliment away, he decided to stop while he was ahead…sort of. "How hard is it going to be for them to find the weapons?"

"By my count we have six, and with them taking turns at tearing it apart, not as long as we need it to be." She picked up her gun then put it down again. "But tracing the vehicle to me will be impossible."

"These guys are trained. They'll have resources." Ward thought about tiptoeing through this, then abandoned the tactic. Tasha was bold and tough. She could handle being pushed around on this topic a bit because the truth was he didn't question her abilities at all. She wouldn't shrink and wouldn't cry.

His biggest worry was that she might kick him in the balls. Good thing he was on the ground.

She snorted. "Rubbish."

The way she said some words kicked his body into wanting mode. Apparently "rubbish" was one of them, which made him question his sanity.

He forced his mind back to the bigger concern. "And then there's the part where you're not at work. On an island this size, that will be noticed. I'm betting you didn't exactly call in sick before heading out here with weapons at the ready."

"That's the real issue. Someone could and will go looking for me."

"Your place is clean?" Had to be. No way would this woman leave important documents or incriminating evidence lying around, but he had to ask. Good or bad, he needed all of the pieces so he could formulate the right plan.

She shot him a look that said "please" but she didn't say it. "Of course."

"We still have these guys in the way." Ward took a long look at the men on the other side of this battle. "Even if I was up for killing them without warning, which I'm not, I'm thinking someone might notice six dead guys around a truck."

She snorted. "You think?"

Time for her to face the harsh reality. "Then your cover is going to be blown. We probably have two days."

Instead of getting angry or flipping into denial mode, she nodded. "Maybe less."

Of course she handled the news fine. That's what she did. Danger didn't appear to shake her. She didn't whine or complain. She adjusted and moved forward.

That didn't mean she liked him. Unfortunately. "Don't blame me for being found out."

"I want to."

Her grumbly voice made him smile. "I can tell."

She looked through the binoculars again. "Is this the part where you tell me to leave the island for my safety?"

"No." As if he'd turn away competent help. The CIA might not approve of a joint international operation on this job because of the little problem of losing sight of the missiles, but his boss wasn't here to whine about protocol, so cooperation was happening. "This is where I point out our window to grab Tigana just tightened. Someone will put the pieces together and figure out you aren't who you say you are, which means figuring out there are people on this island who might just be here for Tigana."

"He could move."

Probably inevitable but not Ward's biggest problem. "Worse, he could start the military coup early, and then we're all fucked, which is why you're staying instead of jumping on a plane back to London."

She slowly lowered the binoculars. "But you CIA guys get the credit, right?"

The woman had a thing about the CIA. Ward vowed to break her of that. "I'm not sure why you think I'm keeping score."

"You want to be able to go back to Langley and tell everyone you took down Tigana." Her expression stayed blank. "Isn't that the goal here?"

She didn't get him at all. "I want to leave this country with the Stinger missiles secure."

The idea of a wild card narcissist using stolen weapons to shoot down planes and destabilize a country scared the shit out of Ward. Once that war started, Fiji would turn into a battleground. Drunk with power, Tigana could go anywhere after that. He held too many missiles to be ignored. This was a die-to-get-the-job-done assignment.

"You're saying the missiles are your only concern here." Her voice dripped with sarcasm.

Looked like they'd need to find some time to work on her trust issue. Damn. "That's the assignment."

"Are we saying the same thing?"

"Yes." And they needed to start now. With the SUV uncovered, the countdown had begun. "We need to get secure so I can contact Ford."

"I have a place."

Now she said that. "Of course you do."

"It's nothing fancy or even all that secure." Wiggling on her stomach, she pulled back from the edge of the hill. "But you could be more grateful."

"Fair enough." But she wasn't the only one who could make demands. "Once our location is secure, you should get ready to tell me why you're so worried about me taking credit for this job."

"I'm not."

No way was she that clueless. "See, Tasha, if we're going to work together, we're going to have to trust each other."

She shrugged as she dragged her body farther out of viewing range. "Not necessarily."

Crawling on his elbows, he followed her. Once they made it down into a dip and were surrounded by trees again, he lifted off the ground but stopped at a squat while balancing on the balls of his feet. "Right. You only need to trust me if you plan to get out of this alive."

"Is that another goal?" After one last scan of the area, she stood up and reached a hand down toward him.

He grabbed on and jumped to his feet. "Always."

"Then tell me the truth." She didn't drop his hand or move back. "How many missiles are we talking about? How big is this threat?"

He tugged her in closer, until they stood only about a foot apart, and rested their joined hands against his chest. "What did your briefing on the weapons say?"

"Tigana got away with at least thirty."

Talk about bad intel. "The number is closer to five hundred."

"What?" Her hand and jaw dropped at the same time. "How did that happen?"

He'd asked that same question a hundred times. He'd nearly been kicked out of a briefing and taken off the assignment after demanding answers. "Don't look at me. I wasn't in charge of guarding the Stingers."

"And if you had been?"

That was pretty fucking easy to answer. "Tigana wouldn't have them."

One of her eyebrows lifted. "You're that good?"

"Yes, I am."

She smiled. "That's strangely comforting."

Good thing she thought so. That might make the next few hours easier. "See, we're getting along better already."

Chapter Six

TASHA DIDN'T DO wonky things. She'd been trained to handle dangerous and avoid dumb. What she wanted to do with Ward involved a lot of naughty, which made even entertaining it shockingly dumb.

Here they were in the middle of a foreign country, tracking down a nutcase holding what she now knew to be a frightening cache of weapons. In good news, no one followed them and her safe house stood well off any trail and miles from where they believed Tigana and his men were holed up, planning whatever awful thing they intended to do next.

Ward wanted to contact Ford. She tried Gareth again without any success. The man had a drinking problem, which was only outdone by his women problem. Tasha hoped he was sleeping off a drunken sex stupor in a bure somewhere.

That left her and Ward with a few things to do. They needed to take an inventory of weapons and map out a surveillance plan that would lead to securing the missiles.

All appropriate to the mission. All made sense. The raging need to jump on Ward and strip his clothes off didn't. With every step they'd taken from the truck site to here, the wanting inside her burned hotter. She chalked the unwanted sensation up to adrenaline or a mix of unspent frustration and energy.

Whatever the answer, it wasn't going away—the jumping inside of her, the churning that had her sneaking peeks at him instead of thinking about ways to take down all of Tigana's men. She needed to burn this off and only knew one way. It was for the job, really. Okay, mostly for her, but still…

She watched Ward walk around the small structure she'd staked out as a temporary hideout weeks ago when she set up her cover. The place had been abandoned, and she paid to keep it that way. Men worked nearby farming kava but stopped their workdays around noon. As the work area moved farther away, the cabin got left behind.

The structure consisted of metal siding tacked and nailed to pieces of wood. Little more than a shed to people outside of Fiji, but not that unusual a dwelling for people in the lower economic rungs here.

She checked it every few days, storing extra clothes and a few supplies in a waterproof bag buried under the makeshift mattress. She kept a cache of emergency weapons outside, hidden up in the trees—a choice that struck her as an unnecessary precaution a few days ago but with her truck confiscated looked pretty smart right now.

Ward did not appear impressed. He had his hands on his hips and wore one of those male frowns that signaled displeasure. "This is basically a lean-to."

Of course, more comments like that, and he might just annoy the desire right out of her. "It has four walls."

"Okay."

Sure, the place measured about ten by ten, but it had a roof…of sorts. It sat away from everything and out of Tigana's targeting range. The least Ward could do was put the ugly American stuff aside and appreciate that they weren't crouched in a hole somewhere. "Sorry it's not a luxury hotel, Your Highness."

He turned his frown away from the building and aimed it her. "What is that supposed to mean?"

"Nothing."

"It's sturdy and efficient. It works for me."

Maybe she'd misread him but she doubted it. "Doesn't seem like it."

"I just thought…"

Whatever came next was going to make her furious. She could tell by his uncharacteristic stammer. "What?"

"You'll get pissed."

Just as she suspected. It was her turn to put her hands on her hips. Her stance now mirrored his as she prepped for the explanation. "You have nothing to lose. You're not exactly saying things that make me like you right now."

"I've stayed in worse. Hell, I've slept in shanties and in an actual lean-to…outside in the snow. In a tree. Once in a net hooked to and suspended from the underside of a mountain." His eyes sort of glazed over as if he were reliving those moments.

Except for that last one, she could relate to all of it. "So?"

"I thought you might pick something different." He shrugged. "That's all."

A red film clouded her vision. She could feel the heat bubble up inside her, and not the good kind. He'd managed to wipe out the need and replace it with fury. "Because I'm a woman and I need comfort?"

He walked over. Stood right in front of her. "See, now. I knew you'd take that the wrong way."

"There's no good way to take it." This was a trigger point for her. She'd dealt with so many men in her field who thought she should strip for the job, be quiet, and act as backup or arm candy. Never mind that she'd saved one or two of those twits from being killed.

"Look, you don't have anything to prove to me." He reached over and took her hand. Uncurled each finger until she no longer held it in a fist. "You knocked me on my ass—"

"Twice." Remembering that put a few more points back in his column. The touching helped too.

He played with her fingers, caressing each one with a light touch. "Right."

"Then I don't get your issue with the building."

He dropped her hand and stepped back. "I'm going to stop talking about that now."

"That would be good." But it wasn't. A chill ran over her as soon as he put distance between them. It made no sense in light of the dripping humidity. She refused to believe the feel of his hand could mesmerize her that quickly, that completely.

The coldness doubled when he walked up the step and into the shack without her. While she watched from the doorway, he spread out a thin blanket over the mats made from pandanus palms and piled up to make a bed of sorts.

"Back to work." One by one he took out his weapons from behind his back and his pants pockets. Some of them were hers, but most were his. "I have two drop sites with more. Neither is near here, but I can get Ford to load up and meet us."

She leaned in the doorway with her arms folded across her stomach, fascinated just to watch the way his lean muscles stretched. That strange kick of interest came back. This time it pounded her, and she had to swallow to keep her voice steady. "Fine."

He glared at her over his shoulder. "Don't do that."

"What?"

"The clipped one-word answers." He swore under his breath. "It's like we're married."

That got her attention. Her arms dropped and she moved farther into the small room. "Have you been married?"

He kept moving around, not giving her eye contact. "For about eight months when I was twenty-five."

"What are you now?" She guessed they were the same age. She might even be a slight bit older.

"Thirty-five."

A light tapping noise against the roof had them both moving back to the door. Blue skies broke through the umbrella of trees above them but a soft rain fell. Typical for the tropical climate. The humidity brought daily rain. This seemed like little more than a short shower, but it would make trekking difficult. Getting in and out in silence and being able to cover their tracks moved to the top of her list of concerns.

But one simple question still stuck in her brain. "Was the breakup her fault or yours?"

His smile came out of nowhere. "I'm divorced. Single and unattached."

"I didn't ask." Okay, she sort of did, but he didn't have to look so damn pleased with himself. Last thing she needed was him thinking she cared about his private life...even though more questions ate at her now.

"I'm happy to share about my private life if you are."

"You are truly annoying." It was either that response or say yes, and that would take them careening straight into the emotional danger zone.

"As if I've never heard that before." He went back to visually cataloging the weapons in front of him.

"But..."

He looked at her with a blank expression. "What?"

If whatever kept pinging around inside of her would just stop, she'd skip this question. But the truth was, she didn't want to. The craving wouldn't stop, and she started to welcome it. "Do not take this the wrong way."

"Cryptic." When she didn't speak up, one of his eyebrows lifted. "I'm waiting."

"This is about adrenaline and nothing else." She sounded like a babbling idiot. For some reason her brain and her mouth were on two different wavelengths.

"What are we talking about?" he asked, his voice echoing the confusion on his face.

It was not as if she'd never had sex. She enjoyed the intimacy and the pleasure—sometimes just for fun, and sometimes because she needed a deeper connection than she got from her run-and-gun lifestyle. Every now and then it was part of the job.

This time would be for her. Just for now. Once and done, and then she could forget him.

She took a deep inhale and went for it. "Take your clothes off."

He looked at her as if she'd lost her mind. "Excuse me?"

"You're attracted to me." Good Lord, now she was waving her hands in the air. Once she realized it, she stopped. Curled her hands into balls at her sides. "I find you...fine."

He covered his mouth and produced a fake cough. She assumed it hid a smile. That was almost enough to make her rescind the offer.

"Really? That's all you can muster?" This time he did smile. "You think I'm fine?"

He was hot and tall and had a face that played in her head long after she closed her eyes each night. And that body. Long and lean with the stalk of a predator. Ward was a man who protected and fought. She got the impression he wrestled demons that had to do with reconciling chivalry and decency with the work they performed.

The combination of all that made her wild with need. "Your clothes are still on."

"Are you saying you want to—"

Since he said the sentence so slowly, emphasizing and halting after each word, she finished it fast. "Shag."

Both eyebrows rose now. "Please tell me that's British for have sex."

"Yes."

He blew out a long staggered breath. "Thank God, because right now my body is in a race to see what will explode first, my brain or my dick."

Uh? "Is that a compliment?"

"Believe it or not, yes." Two steps and he was in front of her with his fingers playing with the small white button at the top of her slim T-shirt. "So, are you talking about now or sometime in the future to celebrate ending Tigana?"

Both. "I need to work off this extra energy and get back in control." She was half-ready to rip off her clothes and throw him on the mattress.

Maybe he knew because he just stood there and stared at her, his gaze not leaving her face.

She stared back.

Just as he started to lower his head, a ripple moved through her. She shoved a hand against his shoulder. "Don't think that I always break protocol like this."

"I don't care if you do." He ripped his shirt out of his pants and whipped it over his head, revealing miles of tanned muscled skin.

"You're taking off your clothes." Not the smartest thing she'd ever said, but it was out there and she couldn't snatch it back.

"Right. You're the boss, remember?"

A shot of regret nearly knocked her over—not at making the pass but at wanting him this much in the first place. Her mind should be on the assignment, not on his chest.

She'd buried this part of her for so long under a pile of work and professionalism that taking it out now made her twitchy. "This isn't—"

His hands went to her arms, and he brushed those palms up and down, soothing her. "Do you want me?"

She couldn't lie. He had to feel it in the tremor shaking through her. "Yes."

"Then stop justifying not working this very second and enjoy. It won't make you less of a professional."

That was exactly what she needed to hear. "Okay."

His hands stopped at her elbows and he dragged her in closer until the heat of his body radiated against her. "You're a stunning woman, and we've been circling each other for days. Honestly, your ability to handle weapons only makes you even hotter in my eyes."

The words spun through her. They felt so good. So right. "Not the way I would say it, but okay."

"You want me. I sure as hell want you. We need to lay low until it gets dark and we can hide our movements better." The corner of his mouth kicked up in a smile filled with promise. "And, for the record, there is nothing sexier than a woman who goes after what she wants."

He meant it. She knew it with every cell inside her.

Screw being overly safe.

Her hands trailed up that bare chest to his shoulders and the sexy dip between his collarbone and the base of his neck. "You're not like the rest of the CIA guys I've met."

He closed one eye as his arms wrapped around her waist. "For the next hour, how about you forget where I work and concentrate on me?"

"That shouldn't be hard." Not with his body rubbing against hers and his erection pressing into the vee between her legs.

"Me wanting you." He kissed her neck. A line of light biting kisses up to the underside of her chin. "Me kissing and tasting you." His lips moved over her cheek.

"Yes." She didn't have any breath so she wasn't even sure if she said the word out loud.

"Me inside you." The intensity of his gaze matched his words. "I can pretty it up but I want to—"

"Say it." She didn't need fancy words. Didn't want them right now.

"Fuck you."

The words, so rough and sexy, vibrated through her. Then his mouth covered hers, and she couldn't say anything. Couldn't think. The kiss, so hot and deep, had her heels lifting off the floor. Every fear and worry fell away as heat washed over her. The touch of his skin, even the pucker of a scar she felt under her fingertips on his back, soothed her.

Ward was a warrior. He fought and would die for his country. She took that same vow. Different country but same devotion. They both believed in something enough to risk everything. Other men said it. From him, she believed it, mostly because he never gave her a speech or insisted on telling her how decent he was. He just acted.

And the man could kiss. Like whoa and damn.

Hot and deep, his mouth traveled over hers. His tongue dipped inside, and the room spun. When she opened her eyes again she lay underneath him. His weight pressed into her, had her squirming to get out of her clothes and touch him skin to skin.

He lifted up on his elbows and braced his body over hers. "I have exactly one condom."

They could make that work. "Find it."

A smile lit up his face, turning him from gruff and hot to irresistible. "It's been in my pocket since ten minutes after we met."

Well, that was pretty damn sexy. "Any chance of you taking it out and using it now?"

His hand tunneled into her hair and held her head still as he lowered his. "I think I can manage a bit more finesse than that."

"No need." She put a finger over his lips. This had to stay mechanical. Two bodies seeking relief and nothing else. "I'm a sure thing here."

"Doesn't mean you don't deserve pleasure." He took her hand and pinned it on the mattress next to her head right before his fingers slid through hers. "We both do."

The next kiss fulfilled that promise. So slow and passionate that it started an ache thumping deep inside her. Need welled up and threatened to swamp her. Much more, and her heart might stop. It hammered in her chest, hard enough to steal her breath.

Then his palm slipped down her body, stopping to cup her breasts before lingering over her stomach and landing on the zipper to her shorts. His fingers went to work. One-handed, he snapped the button open and pulled on the tab. The clicking sound filled the room.

A warm breeze blew over her bare skin as he worked his way down her body. His tongue licked over her stomach as one hand pushed up her shirt and the other dragged her shorts down. Sensations whipped through her. She shifted her head from side to side, trying to zap her mind into working again.

Without warning, the weight lifted off her. She glanced up in time to see the concentration playing on Ward's face. His intense focus stayed locked on her legs as he dragged the shorts the whole way off.

He looked up at her as his fingers skimmed over her, inflaming her. Making her wet. "You call these knickers, right?"

The building heat drove her now. She wanted him inside her. No more talking. No more flirting. Just his body pushing into her.

"You can call them anything you want so long as you peel them off." She lifted her hips to let him know that she meant now.

"Yes, ma'am."

His fingers trailed under the elastic band. He pulled the cotton down and off, never taking his eyes off her. With a gentle touch, he spread her thighs. Then his mouth was on her. With his tongue inside her, he licked and caressed.

So primed, so ready, her hips shifted and her back pressed deeper into the mattress. Without a signal from her brain, she brought her legs in tight against his shoulders. Anything to stop the clenching and tugging inside her. Her body revved up, and tension pounded through her. It was as if a coil kept tightening deep within her, just ready to spring.

"Ward, now." She'd say it in any language he wanted and pulled on his hair to let him know she was serious.

Still, he licked and sucked, bringing her body closer to the edge. The back of her hand fell against her mouth, and she kept it there to stifle the urge to call out his name. When he sat up on his knees, she almost begged him to get back there and go faster.

He needed to get out of his pants first. Thinking to help him, she reached up.

"Ward, here…" She forgot what she was supposed to be doing.

"I can't believe how much I want you." He grabbed her hand and placed a kiss in the center of her palm.

Balancing first on one knee then the other, he managed to get the pants off. He wadded them in a ball, along with his briefs, and threw them to the side.

Turning back, he treated her to a wide-open view of his broad shoulders and the perfect vee of his torso dipping to a lean waist. A thin line of hair started under his belly button and led right down to his erection. Thick and long and pushing against her inner thigh.

She didn't realize he'd grabbed the condom until she heard the wrapper tear. Then he was on top of her again. The friction of their bodies rubbing and brushing had her mind spinning in every direction.

His hands went into her hair, and he kissed her again. Hot, so full of longing. Desire flowed through her and bounced back at her from him. Whatever was happening ran both ways. Electricity snapped between them, and that now-familiar whip of need ratcheted up inside her.

He lifted away from her for a second. Then he was inside her, pushing deep with one long stroke. Her inner muscles tightened as her body folded around him. Their skin touched everywhere. His breathing sped up as his hips moved back and forth, plunging into her in a steady rhythm until she grabbed his ass in her hands and pressed him tighter against her. Then he went wild.

He buried his face in her neck and blew a hot panting breath against her. She felt his muscles tense as he moved. Those shoulders stiffened, and his movements became more intense.

She loved this side of him—demanding and veering out of control.

The need to touch him and tease him with gentle strokes overwhelmed her, but she couldn't follow through. Her body clenched. With each press of his body, she lost a little more air from her lungs. Her fingernails dug into his shoulders as the whirring built, and her head fell back.

"Come for me," he whispered against her neck.

The command took away the last of her control. Her hips bucked, and her arms wrapped him tighter against her. Sweat and heat filled the small room. Their movements beat in time with the rain and drowned out all other sounds.

Just as she felt the last grasp of control leave her, his back stiffened. She feared he would stop, but he didn't. The plunging, the rhythmic in and out continued, as his mouth covered hers. Right as the light burst inside her, he joined her. Control spun away from him, and his body kept moving as small grunts escaped his throat.

Her body shifted and grabbed as the last of the tremors moved through her. Her muscles gave out, and she fell back against the mattress with her chest rising and falling on hard gulps.

He made one last push. His rough groan had her smiling.

It took another minute before he lifted his head and stared down at her. "Damn, woman."

But he didn't get up. He stayed inside her with his arms locked around her.

She slipped her fingers into his hair. Felt the dampness on his skin. "I needed that."

"That makes two of us." The words rumbled in his chest and against her.

Lying there, satisfied and exhausted, she forced her eyes open. They had to get up and plan. Find clothes. Stop touching.

Her last thought was that the man was good at everything.

Seconds, minutes, maybe an hour later, images flashed in Tasha's brain, and she came awake with a gasp. She couldn't believe she'd drifted off, even for a few minutes.

Compounding the sex with sleep…yeah, Ward totally had her off her game. But what a way to go.

She smiled as she lifted her arm to glance at her watch. With that one small movement, she knew. The air in the room felt wrong. Her senses kicked into high gear. Someone watched her. Someone who wasn't Ward.

She jackknifed into a sitting position with the thin blanket pulled over her. She still wore her shirt, but the beating vulnerability—something she hated—wouldn't subside.

"Get up."

The angry voice rolled over her. The scene from earlier replayed in her head. Two men with guns. Slim builds and big weapons. But these two didn't glare. No, their gazes roamed over her. She refused to flinch or jerk the covers. She would not give them the satisfaction of thinking they had her on the defensive.

She was too busy being ticked off. Ward was nowhere in sight. She didn't even see his small pack.

This time she might just shoot him. Of course, she had to live through this first.

"I'm not doing anything wrong." She put a hand against the mattress as her mind raced with possibilities. Maybe she left something that she could…then she felt it. A knife by her side, touching her bare leg. The outline of metal under her hand, just a few layers below. A gun and a knife. Looked like Ward didn't leave her totally defenseless.

Maybe she'd let him live after all.

"Get up," the one on the right repeated.

"No." From here she could launch the knife and get off a shot. The timing would need to be perfect, but she'd practiced this sort of thing over and over.

The one on the right smiled. "Then maybe we'll join you."

When the guy winked, she felt her world tilt. "I'll kill you first."

And she would. Take them out and not think twice. Push down whatever guilt, knowing it was them or her.

The guy took a step closer. "I don't think so."

Before he finished the sentence, the countdown started in her head. She'd take the one on the right first because that guy seemed like he needed killing.

"Drag her off the bed." The one on the left gave the order with a nod of his head.

Go time.

Chapter Seven

WARD WAITED AS the blinding need to attack boiled inside him. He'd gotten up to check in with Ford and heard a noise. He'd been coherent enough to scramble back in time to see these two idiots cross the property line. His skills hadn't failed him, but they had misfired. A few more seconds and he would have been back in the makeshift bed and kissing Tasha again and missed his move—the one where he hid and lay in wait, the element of surprise on his side.

But now it was time. No one touched her without her okay.

Slipping back inside, he had a gun aimed at the back of each of their heads, touching right against their thick skulls before they could lift their weapons. "The lady said no."

The one on the right flinched. "What are you—"

"I will blow a hole through you before you can move your finger to the trigger." Ward's resolve didn't waver. Even a twitch, and they were dead. No questions asked.

The one on the left laughed. Not a real laugh. More of a panicked snort. "We can kill her before you get off a shot."

Not a chance. "Fucking try me."

The one on the left wasn't smart enough to shut up. "Tough man."

Damn straight. "Keep talking, asshole."

Without taking his gaze off the two men and their weapons, Ward's mind went to Tasha. He hoped she understood what had happened. He'd had to get out and get behind them to neutralize them and couldn't take the extra seconds to wake her and explain.

They'd moved a bit faster than expected and had a chance to say all the wrong things to her. Now they would die.

"Honey, did you find what I left for you?" To keep what little of their cover remained, he aimed for sounding loving, which wasn't tough in light of how he'd spent the past hour wrapped up in her.

She lifted the gun. Gave it a little wave. "You mean this?"

That was a good woman right there.

Ward poked the gun harder into the back of the one on the left's head. "Still think you have the advantage?"

"Yes."

The dumb fucker moved. Just a twitch but a fatal one. Ward fired and shoved the guy to the side at the same time. He didn't want the attacker landing on Tasha or even getting near her.

Not that he needed to worry. As he shot, he heard a second round fire from Tasha's side of the room. By the time the banging stopped, both gunmen lay on the floor, bleeding and otherwise making a mess of what was a pretty great hour before they arrived.

Ward checked outside to make sure reinforcements weren't coming to help the gunmen then checked the bodies as his gaze bounced to her. "You okay?"

She held the gun up higher. "Good thing you left this."

"Don't ever say I didn't give you anything nice."

"Very helpful." She rotated to her side and put her feet on the floor. When she stood up, her T-shirt skimmed over her, highlighting the fact she wasn't wearing any underwear.

Half-naked and holding a gun. She was damned near perfect for him.

But nothing else was going right on this assignment. "You know them being here, this far out from Tigana's supposed hiding place, is a bad sign."

"They're scouting." Her fingers fumbled with the hem of her shirt. "Probably searching for the truck's owner."

"Just what we needed, more to worry about."

Her head tilted to the side, and her hair fell over her shoulder. "Before you start thinking you're in the clear or that I'm dropping the subject, do you want to tell me where you went a few minutes ago and why you left without me?"

The question pulled his gaze back up to her face. So did the way she snapped her fingers in front of her. "I was trying to save us both."

"Oh, really?"

No way was he going to be able to shortcut this with some sort of "trust me" thing. The long walk they had in front of them just got longer. "I'll explain on the way."

"Yes, you will." She shot him a you're-not-off-the-hook glare. "On the way to what?"

She wasn't yelling or refusing to go with him. That had to be a good sign...at least he planned on pretending it was. "We're meeting Ford."

They'd checked in at the prearranged time, which was the main reason Ward had woken up before the gunmen came. Ford confirmed the exact location of Tigana's compound. Spotted the series of bures tucked deep into the hills, covered by guards and a newly built wall.

But that wasn't the only news Ford provided. It seemed gossip about Tasha's absence already had raced around the resort. Ward knew that meant they had to move now, ready or not.

"This isn't some dumb male morning-after thing, is it?" Tasha reached for her shorts and held them in front of her.

"It's nighttime." It was a shitty response, but he needed them to move, not hang around and talk about sex. Though if he had any say, they would be having it again and soon. He damn well hoped she felt the same way.

She treated him to an eyeroll, her shorts dangling from her fingertips. "The sex-and-run thing is kind of sad. Please tell me you're better than that."

He understood the conclusion jumping. "I was out there checking with Ford when I heard them. I intended to circle behind them and catch them on the way in, but I couldn't exactly yell or stop and lay out the plan for you. Even with me bolting to get back here, the timing was tight."

She let out a long sigh. "I would have taken care of them."

The prickly thing got old fast. "I was trying to be chivalrous and let you sleep while I made contact with Ford."

"That almost didn't work out for you, did it?"

He decided not to debate that. "Speaking of which, if I had another condom, I'd be all over you. Screw the job."

After a few seconds she nodded. "Okay."

Not exactly the confession of mutual lust he was hoping for. "Okay?"

"I wasn't exactly expecting an audience when I woke up." She took another step and froze before she tripped over the body on the floor. "These two kill the mood."

"Not as much as they should." But her words played in his head.

Through all the death and destruction, all he wanted to do was take her outside for a second round. Proof he had a long way to go toward restoring his humanity.

"Aren't you a dirty boy?" And she sounded pleased at the idea.

This woman was going to be the death of him.

"We finish this job, and I'll show you how dirty I can be," he said.

She smiled. "Promise?"

At least they were back on the same game plan. "Put some clothes on that you can run and fight in before I forget that there are Stinger missiles sitting on this island."

"Killjoy."

"You've got the 'killing' part right. The body count is up to four." He knew it would blow much higher before the night ended. That didn't mean he had to like the idea.

"And there will be more. Every one of them needed to be stopped." She put her hands on his shoulders and peeked around him at the scene on the floor. "I can't let people who get paid by a madman run all over this island."

It was tempting to spin around, to at least lean back against her. He went with turning his head until his lips almost brushed her cheek. "You mean them and not me, right?"

"Mostly." She stepped away from him with a smile.

With every second, his common sense dipped. Much more touching, and they could forget about the assignment and saving Fiji from being held captive. Her smarts and strength and beauty—everything—lured him in.

He cleared his throat in the hope of also clearing his head. "Your clothes?"

"You want me to put them on?" She held up the shorts and made a tsk-tsking sound. "That's new."

Last thing in the world since he met her. "Fuck no."

"That's what I thought." She pointed at the doorway "But it's time, so you go outside."

Shy now? She had to be kidding. She'd been standing there in nothing more than a short T-shirt for a few minutes. "I've already seen everything."

"And if you don't go outside, you'll see it again, which will be a problem for what we need to get done." She shifted to face him and shot a level stare.

The woman was not dumb. Staring at her looking like that made his stupidity meter stick on high. Too much of that, and they'd both be looking for new jobs.

He got as far as the door then turned around to look at her again. Every amazing, half-naked inch. "Have I told you how hot you are?"

"You can tell me several more times on the way to meet Ford."

"Done."

THE HEAT DRAGGED at her muscles as the darkness fell. Forget the idea of a cooling breeze at sundown. Tasha felt the dewiness on her skin and wondered how the island managed to get even hotter without the midday sun.

Baking in a pool of sweat gave a woman time to think. Too much. She'd listened to Ward's explanation of why he left the bed without warning her. She bought it. In his place, she'd have done the same thing—gone out, checked in, then handled the situation. Maintained the element of surprise.

That wasn't what shook her. Her initial reaction to waking up alone should have been a sort of "so what" thing. Instead, she'd been stung with disappointment, and that scared the hell out of her. No way should anything Ward did matter to her…yet it did.

And she needed to say one more thing on the topic. "Thank you."

"For?" He kept his gaze locked on the surroundings. They'd broken through the heaviest part of the tropical forest and circled an open area, careful to stay hidden as much as possible.

Looked like he was going to make her say it. Fair enough. "The assist back there."

He slowed the pace as he glanced at her. "Why do I think it took a lot for you to admit that?"

This is what happened when she tried to play nice. She picked up speed again. "Forget it."

"Whoa." He grabbed her arm and stepped right in her path. "Stop for a second."

No way. "We need to keep moving."

"This will take one second." Without hurting her or pinching, his hold tightened.

The pull had her spinning to face him head-on. Play it off. That strategy hit her, and she went with it. Even used her hand to wave off words and the tension weaving its way around them.

"Not really something a woman wants to hear from the man she's having sex with." The words spilled out, but she didn't regret them. Didn't regret what happened between them either. The intimacy, the touching, the sex. It fueled her, and she would not apologize for that.

His expression didn't give anything away. "I'm going to take the comment to mean you think we should do that again. Good, but do you think for five bloody seconds you could not compare me to every other agent you've ever known?"

She wasn't actually doing that…this time. But the bigger issue was his use of the word *bloody*. The idea of him dragging out British slang drained the last bits of grumbling about waking up alone right out of her. Amusement filled the empty space, and she bit back a smile. "Probably more than five, yes."

He rolled his eyes. "Happy we cleared that up."

The walking continued, this time with the silence stretching between them being more comfortable than before. Maybe it was the heat or lack of a decent meal, but she felt the last of her resistance to him fall away.

She'd once punched a guy right below the belt for calling her a job whore. It was his way of suggesting the sum total of her career goals amounted to sleeping with the right guys to collect information, which was not true— but even if it were, so what? But for some reason, the idiot thought she would appreciate his insight. She went with doubling him over instead.

After only a few days of knowing Ward and less than an hour of rolling around naked with him, Tasha guessed he would swear at the agent and laugh at her solution. She kept it quiet anyway. No need to risk being wrong and rock their newfound equilibrium now that they'd found some.

She swallowed a few times before diving in. "Admittedly, I might be a wee bit defensive."

He didn't look at her. "I'm not responding to that."

Something deep and raw tugged at her. The need to explain, maybe. To make him get it. "And whining isn't my style. As you've pointed out, I tend to get angry at being trivialized, instead."

He glanced over at her. "You think that I don't know how much some men in our business suck? How they use women for information and a bit of fun then look at their fellow female agents as party tricks?"

"But you don't engage in the behavior." She didn't ask it as a question because she knew the answer.

"Never."

The way he jumped to the right response without fumbling around and trying to gauge her reaction killed off some of the anxiety pinging around inside of her. "Some of those guys—not all, of course—view me as their assistant. No one ever asked me to get coffee, but a few came close."

He stumbled over a loose root poking out of the ground but quickly regained his balance. "I'm guessing you outranked those jackasses."

A wave of relief hit her hard enough to shake her balance. When he reached out with a hand on her elbow, she let him help steady her. The flash of chivalry appealed to her. She was starting to think everything about him did.

She mentally walked through this part with some care. "Normally I ignore the nonsense simply by doing my job well."

"Are you saying for some reason I bring out the worst in you?"

Apparently not enough care to get him to stop saying things that sent her temper spiking. "Maybe this worked better when you didn't respond."

He nodded as he kept scanning the area and shifting branches out of their way as they walked. "Right."

A warm breeze punched her face, and the squawk of birds had her glancing up into the thick green blanket of trees. She didn't see anything, but the area burst to life with activity. Not the human kind, but she knew more gunmen lurked out there somewhere. Sooner or later, someone would figure out men were missing or not checking back after their scouting runs, and the tropical paradise would turn into a war zone.

"Gareth." That's all she said. The name of the other man on her mind. The one plunging her into a pool of guilt.

Ward shot her a confused frown. "Excuse me?"

"For the last twenty-four hours, I've assumed he's off having wild sex somewhere, drinking until he can't move." That fit with what she knew about him after their short time paired up together.

She still believed that was the issue. Gareth's file contained more than one warning about his behavior. He'd go on assignment and then go radio silent. She got the distinct impression Fiji was his last shot at holding on to his job. If so, she hoped he had other skills.

"He sounds competent," Ward said without breaking stride.

"That's part of my point. I couldn't get away with that." And that distinction poked at her. Made her dislike Gareth when she barely knew the man.

He'd checked in, then said he was going to take a few hours off. Now, nothing. She'd been about to handle the breach of protocol by hunting his sorry ass down when she found Ward rummaging through her bag. Which reminded her that she had a lot to report at her next check with headquarters.

"Actually, the point is you wouldn't try." Ward steered them farther into the trees and off the path around the open area. "Not your style."

He was right, but still. Men she'd worked with for ten years couldn't reach that conclusion without a diagram and more than a few threats from her. Yet Ward bounced right there.

She didn't know whether to be flattered or terrified. She had almost no experience with either emotion. "You've only known me for a few days."

He shrugged. "I can read people."

Not to point out the obvious… "You didn't know I was MI6 until I drugged you and took your wallet."

"The whole wanting-to-strip-you-naked thing got in my way." He stopped and turned to face her. "Around you my brain cells misfire."

Her stomach did this weird bouncing thing. She half hoped she'd come down with malaria, because if this was some sort of reaction to Ward and his words, she was in deep trouble.

But she had to admit she didn't hate the comments or the strange show of support. "That's kind of sweet."

"Really? Because wanting you this much is driving me fucking nuts." And from the glaring and narrowed eyes, he looked pretty pissed off about it.

"Poor baby."

"My point is I've seen you in action. Most men couldn't take me down. You did it."

She held up two fingers because it was either that or touch him. And she *could not* touch him again. Not now. "Twice."

"Right." He folded his fingers over hers. "Twice."

Something sizzled inside her as she waited for him to drop her hand, to start walking again or reading off tactics for the plan. But he just stood there with his fingers threaded through hers and stared right into her eyes until the intensity had her glancing away.

"You don't panic. You use your smarts. You can hit a target without blinking." His other hand brushed against her cheek. "Trust me when I say I don't view you as window dressing or an extra on this job. I'm betting at some point during the next few hours you'll end up saving my life."

"Is that a line?" Because if it was, she could ignore it. Pretending he didn't exist and didn't affect her were two things she hadn't been able to accomplish.

"No."

So much for pretending. She went into his arms then. Up on her toes until her mouth hovered over his. "Good."

Then she kissed him with all the pent-up frustration that had been building. All the need and the whip of desire. Kissed him until the blood left her head and the dizziness assailed her.

Kissed him deep and long...right up until she heard the approaching footsteps.

Chapter Eight

WARD HEARD A trace, the barest whisper from incoming footsteps. Heard and ignored because this was not the kind of kiss you cut short. You let it linger until it took hold and wiped out everything else. And since he knew that walk and recognized the low whistle as his arranged signal, he knew they weren't in danger.

Ford let out a long exhale as he stepped up beside them. "Good thing I'm not a rabid killer hiding Stinger missiles or anything."

As he lifted his head, the depth of the miscalculation hit Ward. He hadn't thought through the sarcasm or counted on the amount of shit he was going to hear about this. Ford was not the type to let this go. To let anything go.

Ward went for the verbal block. "I knew you were there."

"So did I," Tasha said as she pushed at Ward's arms and stepped out of his hold.

Ford's gaze flicked between Tasha and Ward. "And are we pretending I didn't just see that kiss?"

Ward decided not to sugarcoat this. "Yes."

"Only if you want to live," she said at the same time.

"Okay." Ford clapped and kept rubbing his hands together. "Let's also all pretend we're professionals for a second."

An eerie calm fell over Tasha. "Meaning?"

Ward felt the conversation career right out of control. Ford was a trained killer, but Ward didn't underestimate Tasha. Not anymore. "A little warning here. That word is a trigger for her."

"Want me to shoot you?" Her eyebrow lifted as if daring Ford to say yes. "You know, just to prove how good a shot I am?"

Ford being Ford, he didn't show any outward reaction. "Are all Brits this touchy?"

Before she reached for her weapon and treated them to a live demonstration—and Ward sensed that minute was coming—he plunged ahead. Now would be a good time anyway, since Tasha had made her point and Ford's mind needed to be on something other than that kiss he saw.

"Where is he?" Ward didn't have to say whom. Ford and Tasha knew.

"Here." Ford used his plain black watch to pull up a satellite map of Tigana's outpost, which he'd now confirmed as the target. "I've been doing the head count. We're outnumbered, and they're talking to each other, so they can mobilize."

Ward tucked that last bit of information away for later. "How many men are we talking about?"

With three of them working at top efficiency, they could knock out a small army. But that required information and planning...and time. The last one was proving to be a huge problem.

Tasha had written off Gareth's disappearance to sex and alcohol. Ward hoped that was true, but as the hours passed without communication, he started to think something else was at play. Gareth could be working for anyone, or he could be dead. Ward didn't like either of those options.

Ford shook his head. "Not sure of the exact number of guards, but more than ten are walking around at all times, and Tigana keeps himself surrounded and secreted away."

"Chicken shit." Not as strong as Ward wanted to say but it made his point.

The wind kicked up, and the branches rattled. All three of them shifted into position—backs together and anchored to the nearest large tree trunk for some cover. If a gunman had tracked Ford, which Ward couldn't imagine, or stumbled into their location, they'd be able to track him from all directions.

As the minutes dragged on, Ward kept his arms locked in the firing position as he listened to every sound. He honed in on a few, none of them human.

Once he'd placed them and discounted them as threats, he dropped his hands. "We need a plan."

Tasha jumped in. She looked first to Ford. "You finish the count, and I'll take out a guard. That way I can grab the radio or whatever they're using to talk to one another and gain the advantage."

Ward had to give her credit for guts, but no way was that plan happening. He trusted her to do the work, but there was a better way. His way. "Wrong, you'll go with Ford, and I'll grab a guard."

The glare she shot him could have melted steel. "We're not arguing about this."

She could huff, scream—anything—and still not win this one. "No, Tasha, we're not."

"I don't like it when Mom and Dad fight," Ford said in a childlike sing-songy voice.

Tasha let out one of her the-men-are-driving-me-apeshit sighs. "You're not funny."

Not to be outdone, Ford shrugged. "I kind of am."

Enough. Ward put a hand on her arm and turned her until she faced him. "This isn't a man-woman thing. This is a practical issue. These guys outweigh you."

"Which is irrelevant when I sneak up behind them and shoot them in the head."

Her comeback made his back teeth slam together. "You have an answer for everything."

Ford held his hands together in the sign of a *T* right between Tasha's and Ward's bodies. "Okay, clearly you two have issues you need to work out. Probably has something to do with that kiss, I'm guessing."

"Ford," Ward gritted out.

"Work it all out now, and I'll finish the count." Ford glanced at his watch. "We'll meet back here in twenty. We're coming on morning now and need to move."

"Are you in charge now?" she asked, enunciating each word.

Ward had to smile at that one. He did love to see her stick up for herself and what she believed to be the right thing to do. "You'd be smart to take off instead of answering that."

"Good plan." Ford stepped back and motioned for Ward to follow. "May I see you for a second?"

Ward seriously considered saying no. Between the gunmen and Tasha, the sex and the heat, he had almost all he could handle before rushing in to kill a dictator type. But saying no would only cause Ford to say whatever he intended to say in front of Tasha. Which was likely not a great idea.

After walking a good fifteen feet into the tree-covered area, Ward stopped. From here he could see Tasha as she took over the lookout position. Seemed to be she mumbled to herself as well.

Ward turned to his friend, knowing what was coming next and ready to shrug it all off. "What's up?"

"Are you fucking kidding me?" Ford put his hands on his hips. "Don't play dumb."

Yeah, there were limits, and Ward decided to make that clear right now. "I'd watch it."

"Drop that tone." Ford stood there, fearless and clearly in a fighting mood, as usual. "You need to get your priorities straight. You can't save her, us, and the weapons and this assignment."

"She doesn't strike me as a woman who needs to be saved all that much." Ward could only get so pissed off, as Ford was doing his job. Doing exactly what Ward had trained him to do. That didn't mean he had to love it, and it certainly didn't mean he was going to let Ford take verbal shots at Tasha's competency. "Hell, she handled me just fine, and I'm pretty fucking hard to put down."

Ford's head shot back. "Well, damn."

"What?" Ward ran back over everything he said. Maybe he'd picked up some of her defensiveness and jumped to conclusions too quickly.

"You are into her." Ford lowered his voice to a bare whisper. "I mean, really into her."

Damn it. Not a conversation Ward wanted to have... ever. "It was one kiss."

Ford wore an expression that could only be described as *oh, really.* "So there wasn't more than what I saw?"

Yeah, no way was Ward answering that one. He'd been trained to lie, but Ford had been trained to ferret out the truth. It was a dangerous combination. "Say whatever you're going to say."

Ford shifted until his back was to Tasha. "You have a job to do here, and it's not her."

The comment smacked a bit too close to the truth. Ward had started thinking about her and the job as one thing. In his head he didn't pull them apart or think of her as a foreign agent whose mission might differ from his. They were in this together.

Not that he planned on filling Ford in on that conflict and potentially wrong thinking. Ward would have to work that one out on his own. "Yeah, I know. I'm in charge, remember?"

"Then stop thinking with your dick."

All of Ward's thoughts skidded to a halt. He'd never been accused of that before and refused to accept the charge now. "You have an assignment. Go do it."

"Fine." Ford shook his head. "But you know I'm right."

And the whole walk back to Tasha, Ward feared his friend was correct on this. After confirming the time, Ford left. He had his pack and his watch and his weapons. The guy traveled light. He didn't need more to be lethal. Ward liked that about him.

Tasha watched Ford's retreating back. "What did he say to you over there?"

Ward debated lying but couldn't come up with a reason to do so. She was a smart woman, and he was the one with his priorities all junked up. "That I'm being led around by my dick."

"Huh." Her eyes widened. "You actually told me the truth."

"You asked."

She smiled. "You are a constant surprise."

The comment and the expression seemed to come out of nowhere. He'd half expected anger. He got amusement. This woman had him zigzagging all over the place. "Is that good?"

"I think it might be." Her mouth fell.

He didn't have to ask what drove the reaction. He heard it too. It wasn't as if the person was taking care to be quiet. Pounding footsteps. Steady, almost a march.

"The guard is early." He put a hand on her elbow, thinking to direct her into hiding. She could come out if he needed help subduing…She shook her head and stepped out of his hold. "Tasha?"

"I'll distract him." She put a finger over Ward's lips as her voice dropped to little more than the sound of a breath. "This isn't up for debate, so stop looking at me like that."

A double shot of anxiety and anger hit him as he reached for her hand. "I love your power vibe but—"

"Stop there." She dropped his hand and reached for the gun attached to her waistband, handing it over. "I can't have this visible on me."

"You're pushing it." And by "it," he meant him. He could not let her go out there. This wasn't a woman thing. This was about his personal code. He never handed danger off to other people. He stepped up.

And he needed her safe.

Before he could point any of that out, she squeezed his arm. "Take this guard down without any noise."

Without another word she slipped away. Stepped right out into an opening in the trees. Held the binoculars and walked, looking up as if she were searching for something in the trees. Not doing anything to cover the sound of her steps.

Instead of yelling like he wanted to do, Ward swore under his breath. His instincts screamed at him to dart out and grab her before the guard made a turn and looked in her direction. There was no way the man wouldn't see her then. He walked along the ridge about twenty feet above her and off to the left, facing the other direction. Unless this was his first day on the job, he'd sense her presence. Even someone not trained knew that ticking sensation at the back of his neck that said someone lingered nearby.

They had to play this out now. Bring the guard in closer, lure, and grab. Ward started a mental countdown as he cut through the trees leading away from Tasha. Ducking low and moving with careful steps, he circled, looking to put his body behind the gunman and within striking range.

In his position behind a clump of trees, he watched the gunman glance down the small hill, then do a double take. The guard stared at Tasha, then took off at a dead run. Momentum took him straight to Tasha's position, almost knocking her over.

She jumped back, but he had her. Hands clasped around her shoulders as he yelled at her in a language Ward couldn't make out. But he could see the gunman looked barely twenty. He also carried what looked like a radio.

Time to move.

Ward watched his footing as he skirted around roots and overturned rocks. When this guy showed up early, they weren't in position. That meant trying to launch from behind him from halfway up a hill—not impossible, but Ward needed the guy quiet. He could not allow the guard to fire a weapon or get a shot off.

"I didn't do anything." Tasha held her hands over her head and let the binoculars drop around her neck. She cowered. Sounded panicked.

This was an act. Ward repeated that fact in his mind. She was playing her role.

The gunman kept talking. Fast, red-faced, and out of control, he shoved Tasha on her knees on the ground. *"Kele!"*

Stop. Ward didn't know much Fijian but he knew that word. That meant this guy was a homegrown mercenary or military dropout or something. Tigana didn't bring him to the islands. Ward filed that information away for later. Right now he needed this guy's hands off her.

The gunman pressed on the back of her head, bending her neck toward the ground. His words ran into each other, and his weapon came up.

"Kere veivuke!"

Ward knew that phrase, too. Tasha was calling for help as she covered her head with her arms. Real or not, he was going in.

Crouching low, he stalked in, half at a jog. His steps were rushed, and his shoes slid on the angle of the hill. He made more noise than usual, and his focus stayed locked on Tasha and that gun waving too close to the back of her head.

He'd gotten within ten feet when the gunman turned. His hands started moving first to the gun. Then he reached for the radio hooked to his belt, and Ward pounced. He knocked into the guy's stomach with a grunt and sent them both sprawling.

Ward hit the ground hard. Something sharp jabbed his leg, and the gunman's weapon lodged between them. Ward didn't know which way it aimed as they wrestled in a death match to shove each other's hands away.

They rolled, and Ward's back smacked into a tree. The gunman threw back his head, and Ward knew a cry for reinforcements was coming. Ward cut it off by wrapping his leg around the Gunman's two and flipping him on his back. The energy surge had Ward panting as he slammed the gunman's head against the ground.

Dazed and mumbling, the gunman was running out of steam and his movements slowed. The barrel of the gun pressed into Ward's stomach, and he tried to rip it out of the other man's hands. The gunman turned out to be strangely strong.

Being younger and wiry was an advantage. He morphed from slow to wild in a second. The gunman jackknifed into a sitting position and threw Ward off balance. He hit the ground with a thud, then started scrambling. Legs and arms in constant motion, he grabbed for the gun, but it spun out of reach. They both hit their knees, holding each other back and punching through grunts and groans.

Just as the gunman lunged for the weapon, Tasha's shoe appeared. She kicked it away and aimed one of her own at the gunman's head as he glanced up.

The hesitation was all Ward needed. He wrapped an arm around the gunman's neck and pulled. This wasn't a simple takedown. The goal wasn't to knock him out. This qualified as a wrestle to the death, and the gunman must have known it. He kicked out, and his arms flailed.

Ward did not ease up his hold. The choking sound echoed in his ears as the gunman grasped at his arm, trying to rip and tear his shirt and skin. Anything to fight back as his body shook and his face turned red.

It took only seconds but felt like hours for the life to run out of the guy. Ward held on until the gunman's body spasmed, then went lax. He slid to the ground as if his body had turned to liquid.

Ward sat back on his heels and wiped the sweat off his forehead with his arm. His heavy breathing drowned out the usual sounds of the tropical forest. His mind blanked as he looked up.

Tasha stood there, gun still raised. It took her another second to lower it, and she did it nice and slow. "You're bleeding."

The pain held off until she said those words. The thumping in his leg started a second later. "Damn it."

He tried to get his weight under him, and his knee buckled. Tasha was right there, balancing his body against hers and helping him to his feet with her shoulder under his arm. "Can you walk?"

"Yes." He didn't know if that was true but he needed it to be, so he said it.

"We'll wrap it up and go." No nonsense. Firm and clear, she issued the order as she helped him sit back down on a grouping of rocks.

She left him only long enough to check the gun-man for any signs of life and clean out his pockets. She returned to Ward and handed him the radio.

Blood caked his pants, making the material stick to him. "What the hell did I hit?"

"I have no idea." With a sharp tug she ripped his pants up the inside seam and peeled the cotton away from the injury.

The hiss escaped Ward's mouth before he could stop it. When he looked down, he saw a long cut. Not deep, but it probably needed stitches. Well, that was too damn bad.

The radio crackled. A male voice came on. Then another. Ward cursed his limited knowledge of the Fijian language. Most people here spoke English, and with the tight timeline he'd only been able to pick up a few words of the native language. He shook his head now, trying to ferret out the conversation.

Tasha froze. "Hostage."

Her reaction made him still. "What?"

"They caught a man." She hushed him as she listened. "A foreigner. Someone visiting the island and caught wandering too close to the wall."

Ford. Ward would run on pure adrenaline if he had to now. He pushed his palm against the rock and tried to stand up. "We need to go."

"In a second." She dragged him right back down. "First we need to wrap your leg or you won't be any help to anyone."

"It will be fine." Ward didn't care if that was true or not. He did not leave other agents behind, and Ford was more than a partner on this job. He was a friend, and he would not die while Ward could get him out. He'd crawl over Tigana's wall if he had to.

She grabbed his hand. "You're too close to this to be reasonable. We're doing this my way."

The words echoed what Ford had said about her. Ward didn't like the sentiment any better coming from her. "There's a medical kit in my pocket. You have two minutes, then I'm going."

She opened Ward's utility pants pocket and pulled out a small wrapped package. The kind you took into battle hoping you never had to use it.

"The body count is now five." She made the comment without looking up.

Only one thing ran through Ward's mind. *And Ford won't be number six.*

Chapter Nine

TASHA PACED THE small cleared space in front of the patch of coconut trees as the sun rose. Ford never showed up and wasn't answering the distress calls or whatever Ward kept sending out. And Ward…she waited for him to fall over.

She'd applied the blood-clotting powder and wrapped the cut using the adhesive bandage designed to stop bleeding and minimize infection. But those amounted to temporary measures. He needed a doctor and real medical care. He also needed to put that little black box down before she smashed it under her boot.

"Ward, please." She tried to peel his fingers off the radio, but Ward wouldn't let go. "He's not coming."

"I know." The words snapped out of him. "I'm thinking through the options and am almost ready to go in."

She had no idea what he was talking about. As far as she could tell, he had trouble balancing on the boulder without falling sideways. He couldn't possibly mean... could he? "Where are you talking about?"

"Tigana's compound."

He clearly got hit harder than she thought because even Ward, with his confidence and swagger, couldn't believe he had a chance in this situation. Even if he didn't know, she did. "That is not happening."

"Ford is my partner." He tried to stand up and ended up flinching before falling back down again.

She would have helped him, but maybe a reminder that he could barely walk would help. "And you are injured."

"You know that doesn't matter."

"Says the guy who can't walk." She knew she had the better shot of pulling this off, of at least giving Ford a chance at survival while they extracted the missiles. Now she had to make Ward understand that simple fact. They would shoot him the second he stepped near the gate. He was a threat. The guards wouldn't know what to think about her, and that would be her in.

"We don't have time to argue." He fiddled with the radio on his lap.

Time to go in for the kill. This wasn't fighting fair, but she didn't care—not if it kept him alive, and for whatever reason that had now become one of her top priorities. "So, the 'you're tough' stuff was garbage."

"What?"

"If you think I'm so competent, let me do my job. You create a diversion, take out a few guards, and find a pathway for us to get out." She made it sound easy. Nothing about the Fiji assignment turned out to work as planned.

She lost her partner, inherited Ward and Ford somehow, and was now dragging an injured guy through the equivalent of a tropical rainforest.

"Good plan, except you're not going in," he said.

"You don't have a choice, Ward."

"You think MI6 wins this?"

Since arguing wasn't working, she went to the skill she did better. "Yes."

He looked at her gun, then at her face. "You are not seriously aiming that gun at me."

There was no way she'd shoot anything important. She guessed they both knew that, but he needed to understand how serious she was about this. It wasn't part of an intelligence community turf war. She honestly believed he couldn't function at a high enough level to get this done. "You have fifteen minutes."

"This is ridiculous."

It felt that way, but she refused to back down. Keeping him safe meant everything right now. It was the one pocket she could control. "I'm in charge."

"No you're not." He went from holding the radio to talking into it. "Hello? I found this out here by this big wall. Is anyone there?"

The voice, so unsure and shaky. He sounded lost and confused. The perfect act.

The conversation with the guard continued for a few clipped sentences that ended with Ward being told not to move. He clicked the button off and stared at her.

"What the hell was that?" But she knew. In a way, she'd been played. He might have planned this all along.

"They'll be expecting a man now. That's me." When she didn't say anything, he continued. "You'll be faster. You can create the diversion. Use the intel Ford collected. I'll get you ears in the room, but you need to set the charges. After, I'll get to the bure where the missiles are stored."

She shook off the stunned silence. The urge to strangle him took longer to abandon. "Do we even know which one that is?"

"Ford narrowed it down to two." Ward took off his watch and handed it to her.

She stood there, frozen. His blood still stained her hands, and the image of him going to the ground under that gunman played in her head. But for some reason, he was ready to go again. The idiot. "You're going to get yourself killed. You and Ford. Probably me too."

"We'll see each other again." He picked up her hand and held it. "That's a promise."

She thought about snatching it back but refrained. Mostly because she wanted to touch him right then. The idea that it could be the last time had her trying to swallow over a lump lodged in her throat. "How can you be so sure?"

"We're not done."

IT TOOK ANOTHER ten minutes to get him up and ready. They'd stripped off his weapons. Well, the obvious ones. And he had a mic, the perfect covert listening device. The disc measured no more than the size of a small black dot. It was the only way she'd hear what was happening to him inside.

She prepped the explosives, working fast. Panic drove her. She had the sense that she needed to get him out of there without delay. The churning inside her refused to subside, and if she calculated correctly, they didn't have too long before a storm rolled in. She could smell it on the breeze, feel the heaviness of the air.

"Where's Ward?"

She jumped a good five feet at the sound of Ford's voice. The man had the ability to approach without making a sound. The usual chill that ran over her when someone closed in never happened with Ford. The guy was downright spooky.

When she whipped around, he stood right behind her with his usual scowl. She shot him one right back. "How did you get out?"

His blank expression didn't change. "I don't understand the question."

"You were taken hostage."

"Not me." He shook his head. "A tall blond-haired guy. Scar along the jawline."

"Gareth." Tall and fair and Welsh...and taken. Here she'd been thinking the worst, getting more frustrated with him at every turn, and he'd been snatched. Guilt pummeled her until she had to lean against a tree for support.

"Well, your man is in trouble," Ford said.

She had a feeling that was a vast understatement. "So is yours."

"Meaning?"

"Ward went in after you, or who he thought was you." The assignment had been messed up from the start and had only gotten worse. Two countries on the ground not talking to each other, and now a missing agent and another one on the way to get captured. She couldn't imagine how this could go worse. "And he's injured."

The blood drained from Ford's face. "What the fuck?"

"I tried to stop him."

The unreadable gaze vanished. Anger and worry and a whole lot of other emotions played across Ford's face. "I should think so. It's a suicide mission."

Ford might act nonchalant and have that lone-wolf vibe, but she saw that expression. He cared about Ward. That was a good thing since so did she. "We'll get Ward out."

"The missiles and Ward. We need both."

That was the mantra. The mission came first. But now, faced with losing Ward before she could see if there was anything there worth exploring, she realized her priorities had shifted. She suddenly didn't want to put finding a bad guy before a human life she cared about.

"He comes first," she said, meaning every word.

"No, he doesn't."

He did for her.

THE SHOVE INTO the main bure sent Ward flying into the dining table. He smacked into the wood stomach-first and let out a groan that was more real than acting. He'd have a nice set of bruises there to match the pounding he'd just taken on his ribs and the punches to the jaw.

Tigana's men sure liked it rough, and the sick bastard liked to watch the beatings. Watch and direct, calling out where and how hard to hit next.

Fucking lunatic.

Before standing up, Ward dropped the mic. Not easy with his hands tied together in front of him, but not impossible. Problem was, from all the hits to the head and with his vision blurring, he could barely see it. Still, he managed to cover it with his shoe right before two guys shoved him in a chair and tied his wrists to the armrests.

Tasha would have limited ears in the room, but she'd know where Tigana was and when to detonate. But she had to get inside first. Not an easy task. She'd need one hell of a diversion, as he'd counted just under twenty men, six of whom stayed on Tigana at all times.

The man did like his security. And his food. He sat across from Ward now, picking up these small mesh screens he used to cover plates of food from the flies between bites. "You have made a serious mistake." Tigana spoke in clear English with a slight accent. The years at Harvard had taught him well.

"I found something and tried to return it." Ward kept to his cover story. That's what he'd said into the radio and to the four guards who came to fetch him. Then again to the two who beat the shit out of him.

Tigana sat back, and his chair creaked under his weight. Since arriving on the island, he'd put on a good twenty pounds. Sitting around, planning a country's demise did that to a guy. Now his stomach pushed over the top of his belt and his shirt buttons strained at the holes.

He ran his fingers over his wine glass, tracing the drips of condensation as they ran down the sides. "Where is the woman?"

That was a bad fucking question. If they knew about Tasha, the diversion was dead and so was she. "What woman?"

"You should know her partner likes to talk when he drinks." Tigana put a hand over his glass when one of his servants tried to pour more in there. "It's shameful really."

Gareth. Ward decided to strangle that guy when they met. "I don't—"

"That sort of disloyalty disappoints me." Tigana hesitated before taking another sip of wine. "What about you?"

"I don't know this woman."

He swirled the remaining liquid in the glass. "Lying demands a stiff penalty, don't you think?"

Ward decided to play dumb. No doubt Tigana had a slow, painful death planned. Ward was in no rush to get to that. "I don't know."

"I dislike betrayal." He returned the glass to the table with a soft clink. No anger. Just a monotone voice talking nonsense. "My uncle tried to betray me, and I burned him alive."

Ward knew. The entire intelligence community knew. He'd seen the file. Understood the uncle had been working with the CIA. Working with anyone who could take out Tigana. "Please let me go."

"Do you see that?" Tigana pointed behind Ward.

Ward tried to turn his head but couldn't see anything except the open walls and mass of greenery outside. He scanned what he could see—hand-carved furniture and bouquets of wildflowers on a few tables. Tigana had set up the bure to mirror an expensive resort.

Tigana nodded to his men, and Ward felt the room spin. Two guys shifted his chair until he saw directly behind him. The prone body, or at least his legs, sticking out from behind an overstuffed couch. "Your friend's partner screamed and begged. Very disturbing. I wonder if you will do the same."

"Is he dead?" Ward forced his question to rise at the end like people in a state of panic tended to do.

"Very." Tigana rested an elbow on the armrest and flashed the expensive rings on his fingers. "Now, tell me who you work for."

Ward flipped from one cover to another. This one worked on Tasha, at least for a few days. "A financial company back in the United States."

"This grows tiresome." Tigana let his arm fall against the table with a hard smack. "Which government?"

"I'm a businessman here on vacation." Ward rushed his words and let fear seep into his voice.

He'd been searched for weapons, but the idiots left the pen in his pocket after being so excited about finding the wallet full of fake documents. He moved his hands, trying to loosen the ties, pulling and tugging with as little movement as possible.

"I don't think you are." Tigana nodded to one of his henchmen.

The man brought over a long knife with a serrated edge. One look had adrenaline surging through Ward. Not that he didn't know fear. He understood the sensation but channeled it into action, as he'd been trained to do. The message on the loop at the back of his mind said *at least Tasha is safe outside*. At some point, that began to matter more than almost everything else.

"I like knives." Tigana ran his finger over the side of the blade. "My father taught me to use them when I was ten."

Ward didn't talk because it looked as if Tigana had gotten lost in his story. Not that he needed to tell it. Ward knew all about Tigana and his entrance into killing. Age ten when his father challenged his manhood. The family really was awful. Almost made Ward appreciate the strict no-room-for-mistakes household he grew up in.

"I'm going to show you what I did the first time a man lied to me." Tigana chuckled. "Maybe that will help your memory."

Ward tensed as two men grabbed him from behind. One held a gun to his head as the other untied a hand. Stupid fucking move, but he'd take it. With one hand free he could grab a gun, strangle someone.

The tie had just been loosened when another man came into the room. He looked like all the others, twenty and holding too many weapons for him to handle effectively. Apparently there was no end to the parade of disaffected men looking for a new leader here on Fiji.

"Sir, we have her."

Ward's stomach dropped. Fell to the damn floor. The buzz of energy that had been pulsing through him, preparing him, turned to stinging anxiety. There was only one her.

As soon as he thought it, three men dragged Tasha into the room. Without blinking she stood in the same gray tank and olive cargo pants she'd changed into after they had sex.

"Well, well." Tigana stood up and pulled on the waistband of his pants, but his belt didn't go one inch higher. "We've been waiting for you."

The guard who made the announcement about catching Tasha spoke up. "She says she's his fiancée."

Tigana turned his feral smile back on Ward. "I thought you were here on business."

With the guard having loosened the tie, Ward was so close to breaking free. Doing so had become imperative. He had to get free and get to her before Tigana put the plans he had for her into motion. "Vacation."

"Come join us, my dear." Tigana pulled out his chair and motioned for her to sit in it.

She didn't really have a choice. Between the bindings securing her and the guard holding her, she had to go where they put her, and they dumped her in the chair Tigana assigned.

"You are just in time."

Her eyes narrowed just a fraction. "For what?"

"To hurt your fiancé." Tigana nodded.

Before he could even focus, Tigana grabbed Ward's hand and flipped it palm up. He heard Tasha scream as a blade flashed and the knife came down. He'd been shot and stabbed, usually in the heat of battle or during an attack, so he didn't feel the wound until after. This time he saw the blade fall. Watched inch after inch disappear into his palm and pin him to the table.

Pain rolled over him, but he blinked it all away. He had to stay awake and in fighting form for her. Then he heard a noise and couldn't figure out if something exploded in his head or in the yard. Either way, it meant he had to remove the knife and get them the fuck out of there.

Chapter Ten

THE ROOM BROKE into chaos. Men ran around shouting and yelling directions. Tasha heard a mix of languages and tried to break them apart. Her concentration kept bouncing, and she couldn't stop staring at Ward's hand.

His fingers curled in, and he leaned forward as if trying to ease the pain. Blood pooled on the table, and a blade stuck in the dead center.

She possessed a high tolerance for awful things. That was a mandatory characteristic for someone in her job. But this was sick and vicious, and she ached with the need to help him.

A group of men grabbed Tigana and shielded his body with theirs. No one seemed to notice her or care. Two guards lined up at the windows in shooting position. She knew they were wasting their time. Ford had just blown up one bure, and the second would explode any minute now. That should send the rest of them scattering.

Tigana grabbed onto the thick post that served as part of the doorway. He glanced over his shoulder at her, then at Ward. He got his guards' attention. "Kill them, then come."

The order had been handed down. Ward shifted in his seat, but his bound hand kept him trapped there. No one had bothered to tie her up. It was one of the perks to her size and sex. Some men thought she couldn't fight back. They would learn.

She waited until one of the men closed in. She knew what she had to do and glanced at Ward.

He nodded. "Do it now."

The guard came within striking distance, and she let loose. She was up on her feet, reaching across the table. The knife slid out of Ward's hand. He flinched but didn't make a sound as he used the bloody blade to cut his other binding. The only noise came from his chair slamming against the floor as he stood and stepped back.

But she was already moving. With one pivot, she stabbed the guard in the chest and ripped the gun out of his hand. A second stab and he went down, just as she fired on his friend.

When the firing and yelling cleared, both men lay crumpled at her feet. She only cared about the one standing across from her, pale as he ripped the bottom on his T-shirt with his uninjured hand and wrapped the wound.

"Ward." She rushed over.

She expected him to at least double over. Not him.

He leaned against her for a second, then straightened again. "We have to move."

It was the right answer. The one pertaining to the job. His voice was rough, and he was somehow ready to go. He talked about her toughness being hot. He was the one shooting off the hotness scale right now.

Except for the blood. It ran everywhere. That would give away their position and eventually weaken even a man as tough as Ward.

"Here." She took what looked like a clean napkin off the table and carefully wrapped it around his makeshift cotton bandage.

"Can you hold a gun?" She hated to ask, but she had to know.

He looked at the bloody bandage. "Not with that one, but I have experience with the other."

"Of course you do." That came with the training. Still, she'd never been able to master that skill. At the very least, his shot would suffer. That had the potential to leave them one agent down. But they did have one other weapon. "Ford is alive. He's the one who set the charges."

Ward gave a curt nod. "How many men do we still have out there?"

She loved his ability to stay on task when the pain had to be plowing him under. Another man would have fallen down or passed out. Not Ward. "We took out six on the way in. Ford has probably handled others."

"Tigana? That fucker is mine."

For some reason the mix of anger and determination in Ward's voice made her feel better. "Let's go."

WITH EVERY BOUNCING step, his hand throbbed and the pounding in his head doubled. Ward needed to stop and sit down, but that wasn't an option. He'd gotten out of that room—she'd gotten him out—and now he had to finish the job. If he had to carry the missiles out of the compound one by one under his arm or by dragging them behind him, he would.

They had to snake their way out of the main grouping of bures first. Armed men ran around, and smoke filled the air. Whatever Ford had blown up had an impact. Fire raged in two vehicles, and bodies littered the ground. With a loud whoosh, the thatched roof of one bure went up in flames.

Still they ran. Choking on suffocating air and fighting their way through trees and a blanket of smoke. Cutting across the lines of trucks and through the stacks of boxes. He glanced at them, but they were the wrong type. He needed five-foot-long aluminum green cases. Those would be the Stingers, and with the number he had, they were stacked somewhere.

He'd trained his weaker arm for years and now had solid aim with a blade. His gun use hadn't fared as well. He could shoot, but the aim suffered. But he could stab and he planned to do just that.

She glanced back at him over her shoulder. "Are you okay?"

"Stop asking." He tried to close his injured hand, and a shock of pain spiraled through him. He closed his eyes and forced his body to stay upright as he swallowed back the bile racing up his throat.

The only good news was she missed it all. She turned forward again with him to the side and slightly behind her.

"You make it hard to care about you," she said.

"So I've heard."

She shot him another glance as they reached the end of a building. A man came flying around a corner and ran straight into her. The guy bounced back with a stunned expression.

Ward slammed him in the forehead with the blade before he could reach for the trigger. The body dropped, and Tasha skidded to a halt in front of it.

"I think we're up to eight between us, plus the ones I eliminated with Ford." Without missing a beat, she reached down and pulled out the blade. After a quick wipe on her pants, she handed it to Ward.

"There's only one man I want in all this." And Ward vowed to get him.

Up and going again, they headed for the building where the guards still stood—a place that looked more like an oversized garage next to what Ward believed to be a hangar of sorts. Not that anyone could land a plane in this wooded area close to the ocean.

She stopped behind a truck and waited, and Ward joined her. Ford was out there somewhere. The second after Ward thought it, a new explosion went off about fifty feet behind him. Heated air blasted into his back and singed his clothes. One minute he stood, and the next he was on his knees with Tasha beside him.

Smoke rolled over them as a series of crashes and bangs had them ducking. More bodies fell to the ground.

One person raced around on fire while another tried to put out the flames. It was a horrible display but necessary. Not quiet, and the entire Fijian military would soon come running, which meant they had to pick up their pace.

"What happened?" Tasha pushed off the ground and sat up.

"Ford got a little close with that one." But Ward was focused on one thing now. Someone who filled his thoughts until Ward wanted to carve out a piece of his brain to kick him out. Tigana. It didn't matter to Ward that his hand didn't work and might never again.

With one final scan, Ward took in every inch of the compound. A circle of bures surrounded by one larger one. Outbuildings that looked like kitchens and a shed. There were buildings scattered around and people running everywhere. Structures on fire and crumbling.

But one building stood out, untouched and secured. "That has to be it."

Trucks pulled out and took off in different directions. He strained to see if Tigana sat in any of them and didn't think so. "Where did the man go?"

"I didn't see." She tapped on Ward's watch then ducked when another explosion went off somewhere behind her. "Can you reach Ford?"

"I wouldn't be able to hear anything he said." Ward eyed the building one more time. A few of the guards met together by the double front doors, probably to discuss whether or not to abandon their posts. That meant some position was uncovered. Ward vowed to find it. "We need to circle around back."

They'd just taken off when the shooting started. They zigzagged until Ward realized they were not the targets. Ford drew their fire, madman that he was.

The steady jog had Ward's hand going numb. The pain had subsided until he lost all feeling in his fingers. He knew that was a really bad sign, but it might be what he needed to survive this—what could be his last mission.

They got to a side window. After a quick check inside, he lifted Tasha as best he could and her athletic ability handled the rest. He watched her slide through. Seconds ticked by, and nothing. She didn't call out. No gunfire. A door halfway down the building opened, and she peeked out. He didn't question his luck. Not having to drag his body up the side of a building with one working hand appealed to him.

They walked through a small room where paperwork lay scattered on the top of every surface, but no missile boxes. Every step echoed through the two-story warehouse, but no one tried to stop them.

Ward took a deep inhale and said the sorry truth. "That was too easy."

"No kidding."

They both stayed alert as they walked. When they got to a locked door, Ward could feel it. The weapons they needed were on the other side. Maybe not all five hundred, but he sure as hell hoped so.

The knob turned in his good hand, and the feeling of dread settled over him. Any job that went as planned ended in a nightmare. He'd been doing this long enough, since straight out of college, to know.

He opened it slowly.

The thunder of noise hit him first. The roar of engines and a *thwapping* sound. Tasha's eyes narrowed, and she peeked inside. Then she went in.

He followed, keeping his body low and dodging from stack to stack of green boxes. "The weapons."

She kept moving, heading toward the opposite end of the long building. "Some." She pointed at the two open garage bays at the far end of the room. "They're loading them up."

"Looks like they're taking the guns on the road." That was the nightmare scenario.

Tigana had to be stopped today. No matter the sacrifice.

They edged behind a stack of crates. Six guys worked in unison, loading the missiles into two trucks. The engines were on, and drivers sat ready. This they could deal with. The other noise was the problem.

"He has a helicopter," Tasha said.

Ward had already put those pieces together and he hated the conclusion. "Tigana is on and ready to go."

"Good thing we're sitting in a room full of surface-to-air missiles."

He liked the way she thought. "Right. We load these on our shoulders and fire."

He was half kidding, but it might come to that. But neither one of them commented on his ability to balance a thirty-pound weapon with one hand. It didn't matter. Somehow they'd get it done.

"Put the weapons down." The male voice came from behind them, and then another joined in.

They had company. Armed company.

Ward felt a punch of guilt. He hadn't heard them and couldn't help her now, not the way she needed backup. Without his full strength, he had to rely on his brains.

After a nod to Tasha to signal it was okay to stand up straight, Ward held up his hands. "Hold on. We're fine."

"Don't move."

But Tasha was already shifting. She had a gun tucked in front of her. Another appeared in her other hand. As she turned, shots rang out. A shout lodged in his throat as he waited to see her fall. Flashes of the past week ran through his brain. Tasha at the bar. Walking beside him. In bed.

He could not lose her now.

Almost in slow motion, he pivoted, ready to throw his knife, his weight. Anything. By the time he turned, he saw only one man standing there—Ford. He'd dropped the other two, and Tasha stayed on her feet.

Ward wanted to hug her, kiss her. But they had to finish this job first.

"Ready to launch a few missiles?" Ford asked.

"We have to shoot through those guys first." Tasha gestured to the men standing outside loading the trucks. The noise must have drowned out anything because they moved fast and didn't even glance back.

Refusing to be left out, Ward held out his good hand. "I need a gun."

Ford stared at the bandaged palm. "Really?"

"I can hit something." Ward's left-handed shot wasn't perfect, but it was probably better than that of most normal people.

Ford snorted. "Just don't hit me."

Guns in hand, they started the countdown. On three they took off, gliding through the warehouse with Ford down the middle and Tasha and Ward on the two sides. They hit the end and opened fire. The men around the trucks fell one after the other in boneless heaps. Ford raced to the front of the trucks and took out the drivers as the *thwapping* sound grew louder.

Tasha and Ward looked around the corner. There it was: a helicopter loaded down with people and boxes. Ward had no idea where the man planned to go, but he'd stop it if he had to jump on board and throw people off.

"We have another truck. It's riding low." Tasha pointed in the distance.

"It's full." It looked as though one truck had gotten off and was trying to navigate the rocky dirt road that headed to the water, which led Ward to one conclusion. "He has a boat waiting."

Tasha shook her head. "Damn."

Ward didn't know how he knew, but he did. "Help me with the missiles."

"Are we really going to fire one?" she asked.

"We're going to need two." He glanced down at his useless hand. "And I'm going to need you to help me."

Working in silence, they uncrated the weapons. Ford came back, his eyes wide.

Tasha shook her head. "You're too excited."

"No such thing," Ford said as he set his up.

A few minutes later, they were up and ready to go. Ford targeted the truck. Ward had the helicopter. Normally he would throw the weapon on his shoulder and go. He'd used it before and had no trouble, but he couldn't maneuver anything and he was losing blood with each passing second.

Tasha helped shove it on his shoulder. "We're doing this."

It was all a matter of infrared and motion sensors now. Ward widened his stance, ready to fire when the bullets started raining down. The shooter positioned on the helicopter fired as the bird rose into the sky. Other men, those left behind but still shooting, came around the building. They were out in the open and taking fire from all angles.

"Go now!" Ford yelled as he launched.

Ward pulled the trigger, but his strength failed. Between the smoke and the injury and the bullets, he couldn't get the shot off and risked letting Tigana escape. Then Tasha was beside him with her arm wrapped around his waist and her hand gripping the trigger with him.

"Now, Ward." She shouted the order into his ear.

The truck exploded in the distance as Ford landed his hit, then turned his sights on the shooters. With his missile launched, Ward could only wait. A second later, the helicopter burst into a fireball and debris fell from the sky.

Ward tried to run to safety, but his legs gave out. He fell to his knees as Ford provided covering fire. By the time the booms and crashes stopped, half of the compound was on fire and none of the shooters remained standing.

Ward lifted his hand to touch Tasha's shoulder and saw the napkin was totally soaked in blood. He wanted to say something to her, but the world started to blink out on him. His final thought was about being swallowed up by black smoke.

Chapter Eleven

TASHA STOOD AT the closed door for a solid five minutes. The smells of the hospital wound around her. Metal and antiseptic. Cleaning supplies and a certain staleness that came from the lack of fresh air.

Though if you had to be in the hospital, Hawaii was not a bad place to recuperate. Leave it to Ward to end up in a room there.

With a big inhale, she shoved the door open and stepped inside. Ward's head came up, and Ford stopped talking.

She got a welcoming smile but not from the man she expected. Still, somehow she kept walking until she stood at Ward's bedside.

"Hello." Ford came around to her side and kissed her on the cheek.

It was the weirdest welcome ever. The man she needed so much, the one she dreamed about and spun fantasies around, stared at her with a blank expression. He acted as if he barely knew her. He seemed so disconnected that she wondered if his CIA boss hid in the corner watching.

She plastered a smile on her face as her gaze traveled over the covers to Ward's bandaged hand then to his pale face. Even her fake expression faltered then. "You look like hell."

"Thanks." That was it. He didn't say another word.

The moment couldn't be more awkward or tense. She almost backed right out of the room and kept walking until she hit water.

Ford smiled at her. "He passed out on the job, and it pisses him off."

"I'd lost a lot of blood."

"Splat." Ford made a dropping motion. "Fainted."

She listened to the banter. Heard them joke. She was happy for them and the friendship, but this is not the conversation she wanted.

Ward turned his head on the pillow and looked at Ford. "Go away."

"Right. I'll go find bad coffee." Ford gave Tasha's arm a gentle squeeze. "By the way, nice job."

"Thanks." The compliments had her reeling. He hadn't said two words to her in the field. Now he acted like they got along.

He winked. "For a girl."

That was more like it. This she could handle. "There are needles everywhere. You should remember that."

"Don't have to tell me twice." Ford waved as he walked out. "I'll be back later."

Then the silence fell. Neither one of them said a word until Ward finally broke in. "You scared him."

She shrugged. "Comes with the job."

"And you're impressive at it."

Admiration was not really what she was looking for here. She'd hoped they could skip over this part and talk about something else. Like how her world crumbled when that knife went through his hand. How she held him as US military recon crashed into the complex and confiscated the stolen weapons. She hadn't even known they were stationed nearby, waiting.

But mostly she wanted to talk about seeing him again. He kicked something to life inside of her. A light clicked on and she wanted to explore that, but he'd gone into shutdown mode, and she had no idea how to break through or if he even wanted her to try.

"Apparently not, since I'm being called home to account for Gareth and explain why I was working with you and firing missiles." She half expected to be fired for doing her job. The grumbling and strange buzz had grown so loud that she didn't know what she was going back to the office to find.

He cleared his throat. "Are you leaving for London soon?"

She wanted him to ask the right question. Say the right thing. "I live in England, so yes."

"Thank you." He held out his hand. Actually laid there and acted as if they were business acquaintances.

She stared at his palm. "Are you kidding?"

He let his hand drop. "I didn't want to presume."

There was nothing. The flirting was gone. Whatever feelings he'd had disappeared. Maybe it all had been an act for the mission. If so, he was damn good because he had her believing. Had her hoping.

This she couldn't do. She was not the breakdown type. She didn't fumble over a guy. And if she was going to start now, she would do it in the shower in her hotel room.

That meant she had to get out of there. She couldn't stand there and pretend not to care.

She leaned down and kissed him on the forehead. "Good-bye, Ward."

"You're leaving?"

She had to if she wanted to preserve any sense of dignity. "Try not to get yourself killed."

"I can't promise that."

She threw him one last weak smile and walked out. Stepped away from something she thought had sparked but clearly only ran one way. Now she had to forget it all. She looked down at her purse and the airline ticket sticking out of the side pocket. She didn't need that later flight now. It was time to get back to her life.

She got as far as the elevator before she ran into Ford. He was coming off, and she was getting on.

He saw her and stepped out of the car, blocking her ability to move around him. "You're going?"

Her chest hurt. Hell, everything hurt. "It's time."

The doors closed behind him and she reached around to hit the down button. He watched her, and she stared at the closed doors, willing them to open again.

Just as the bell dinged, Ford started talking again. This time in a whisper. "He's not a jackass."

"What?" She stepped into the car but held the door.

"It's the hand and feeling useless."

"In other words, it's not about me." Yeah, he'd made that clear. She'd been thinking about him, worrying, and ignoring what she needed to do in terms of a debrief for work. He...well, she didn't know what he was doing because he clearly didn't want to share.

"He's been talking about you nonstop."

She punched the button for the lobby and watched the doors begin to close. "Nice try, Ford."

"I'm serious."

And she was done. "Good-bye."

WARD STOOD OUTSIDE the office and flexed his messed-up hand. Three months had passed, and he still didn't have feeling in two of his fingers. The slice through the tendons and everything else in there had destroyed his grip, leaving it hard for him to close his hand. He'd tried shooting but felt the pain from his palm to his feet. The injury hurt, being taken out of the field pissed him off... losing Tasha crushed him.

But he was hoping to fix that part today.

He knocked once and went in when he thought he heard a faint noise on the other side of the door. He shut it behind him and looked around the room. Blue walls and a big desk. Files stacked on every corner and more on the small conference room table by the door. The one problem was the lack of humans.

He heard an intake of breath and looked around. Tasha stood there, by an open closet, gawking at him. And not in a good way.

"Why are you here?" she asked in a flat voice.

He had hoped that would be obvious since one of the files in this office should be his résumé. "For a job."

"What?" The door clicked as she shut it and moved around to the front of her desk.

Seemed they were not on the same page. He took the blame for that. She came into his hospital room back when he was still in pieces and he'd pushed her away. Dumbass that he was.

"The Alliance." He dropped the top-secret name and waited.

She didn't break her stare. Didn't talk either.

"Okay, I'll keep going, and you can jump in when you want to." He inhaled, trying to calm whatever bullshit was jumping around in his stomach.

It would have been easier if she didn't look like that. Her wavy blond hair fell over her shoulders and...did she have a tan? Where the hell did someone get a tan in London?

"Thanks to our venture and us almost blowing up Fiji by accident, the CIA and MI6 are starting a joint project. Black ops. Limited oversight. Not bound by the rules of either organization." She hadn't blinked, and that was starting to freak him out so he wrapped it up. "That's why I'm here."

Her gaze went to his hand then bounced back up to his face.

He decided to fill in that blank since she'd apparently lost the power of speech. "I'm out of the field. Can't be on operations if you can't feel your hand or shoot a gun. But I'm not here for that position. You need people to run the projects who have experience in MI6 and the CIA. I'm here for the CIA, obviously."

She leaned against her desk in her gray pantsuit but didn't show any other visible signs of life.

Now he was getting worried. Maybe Ford was right that he'd waited too long. Three months without communication was a bit much. In Ward's head it made sense. He'd come to her as whole as possible. But now he thought he might have fucked up.

"Any chance you can say something?" Though he was starting to worry about what that might be.

"You want to work for me?" she asked.

Not exactly the I'm-miserable-without-you statement he was hoping for, but at least she said something. That was a start.

But this part could get bumpy. "Not really."

Her eyes narrowed. "You don't want a job? I'm confused."

This is not how he wanted it to play out, but when a guy was desperate, he did desperate things.

"I want to be with you. To date you. To see you. The job is the practical part, but it happens to put me near you all the time." He took another deep breath. "Tasha, could you—"

Color moved into her cheeks. "You practically ran me out of your hospital room with your lack of interest. You don't call or answer my texts." She ticked off his sins on her fingers. "Now you want to date?"

This Tasha he recognized. Full of life and fighting back. This is the woman he couldn't forget and needed so much to forgive him. "It sounds ridiculous when you say it like that."

"Good-bye, Ward." She walked around her desk and sat down. She snatched up a pen and held it tight enough to break it in half.

Yeah, that wasn't happening. He deserved to be written off, but he had to keep fighting. "Can I just explain?" When she didn't say no right away, he raced ahead. "I spent my entire adult life in the field. Undercover operations is all I know. Losing that felt like I lost everything I am. Everything that mattered."

Her grip tightened, then loosened on the pen. "The use of your hand could come back."

"Never fully. Never enough. There's too much damage to the nerves and muscles."

"So I'm the consolation prize?"

This got all screwed up, and now she was thinking about work when he wanted her thinking about him. He doubled back.

"Okay, I totally fucked this up." He came away from the door and around to her side of the desk. He knew it was an invasion of her space, but he needed to take this one shot. "Let me try again."

"I don't think that's a good idea." But she didn't kick him out or order him to leave.

So, he pushed it one step further and slid his thigh on the edge of her desk. "I couldn't help you. If something happened to you in that room when Tigana left and ordered us killed or in that warehouse or while we were out on the tarmac and gunmen opened fire, I couldn't have saved you."

Something in her eyes softened. "I don't need you to save me."

"I know, I just…" He wiped his hand through his hair and tried to find the right words. "You left my hospital room, and it felt like a kick to the gut. I have missed you every fucking day since."

Her eyebrow lifted. "You never called."

He wanted to gloss over this and forget it but he had to put it out there. She deserved to know it all. "I went to physical therapy, and it sucked. I couldn't even squeeze a damn rubber ball at first. Still really can't hold one in a tight grip, but at least I can move some of my fingers. But that's after months of sweating it out, dealing with scar tissue, and fighting through nerve pain."

"Ward—"

"The only thing that kept me going was following you from a distance, which wasn't easy thanks to your security clearance and your country's insistence on you not being my business."

"From a distance…what does that mean?"

This part made him sound like a stalker. He'd told Ford, and Ford told him to either get over her or buy a plane ticket. Ward went with the latter. "I know you lobbied for the Alliance. I know it's your baby, and it is so smart and…well, you."

"Working together is the right answer," she sputtered. "For the UK and US, I mean."

"I know you don't get to pick the CIA person. That person is more or less assigned, and all you get is veto power." God, he needed her not to exercise that veto. He hoped that being British, she didn't even know what a veto power was.

"Uh-huh."

She sounded angry, but he saw something. Maybe that old spark. That light that filled her face and made him stupid. "You're getting me as the CIA head."

Her eyebrow rose. "You think you decide?"

He detected a thread of amusement in her voice, so he kept going. "Well, I want to date you and live in the same city as you and all of that stuff, and if you hire me, I'll have a job. That will make paying for dinner easier."

She had her armrests clenched in a death grip now. "Why?"

He didn't pretend to be confused. "Because I think about you all the time. Because I'm miserable without you."

"Leaving you was the worst thing." She shook her head as her words cut off.

"I close my eyes and you're there. I pick up my phone and play that message you left months ago just so I can hear your voice." Because he couldn't stand not touching her for one more second, he stood up and reached down to drag her up beside him. "For the longest time, I was sorry you saw me weak."

Her head tilted to the side, and all traces of anger fled her expression and body language. "Ward, that's not true. I never viewed you that way."

"Now I'm sorry I ever let you leave." He slipped his fingers through her hair. "Please give me a chance to prove I'm not an ass."

"You're not." Her hands found their way to his waist and rested there. "And you are not weak. You might actually be the toughest guy I know."

"Then you should take a chance on me."

She winced. "You understand that if you get this job, I'll be your boss."

"Doesn't bother me." He ducked his head to meet her eye to eye. "You being strong and smart and beautiful doesn't threaten me."

"I believe you." She nodded. "You showed me that several times."

Hope grabbed on inside of him. She wasn't pushing him away or making him pay for what happened. She might not understand. It could take weeks, maybe even months for that, but he'd wait. For her, he'd learn to be patient.

"And I checked. I can date the boss." That was a deal-breaker for him. That and bringing Ford along with him.

She pulled back, and her mouth dropped open. "What?"

"That was one of my conditions when I said I would take the job."

She shook her head. "What are you talking about?"

"I told the higher-ups that I was already falling for you and would not stop just because I was in an office and attending meetings with you." It was his turn to wince. "I also admitted that you weren't all that fond of me right now, so I had to work to put us back together again."

"Falling for?"

He decided it was a good sign she grabbed onto that. The way her fingers tightened on his skin probably meant he had a chance, too. "That old guy with the heavy British accent nearly spit up his tea, but he got it."

"I'm trying to imagine that scene."

Her wrapped his arms around her and pulled her in tighter against him. The feel of her body along his eased some of the constant burning in his gut. "Look, I can follow orders at the office. So long as at home I get to be in charge, and by that I mean in the bedroom."

"That sounds…" She smiled. "Wait, at home?"

"Did I forget to tell you I don't have a place to live?" He wanted to be in every part of her life. He could wait on some, and would, but he was tired of sitting around not saying anything.

"You're being pretty presumptuous." Tough words, but her hands slid up his back.

He cupped her face. "I want it all."

"Are you sure?"

He balanced his forehead against hers and inhaled her scent. "Any chance you missed me?"

She placed a quick kiss on his lips. "Every single day. I was sick with it."

"Thank God." Relief washed through him. He closed his eyes to get his bearings, and when he opened them again, she was staring at him.

"Nice."

"We can make this work." He knew that was true. Believed it with every cell and every muscle. "Because honestly, I've tried living without you and I don't like it."

She sighed. "I can be difficult."

"I think you're sexy." And to show how much he meant it, he kissed her. No soft and sweet. No, this was deep. Full of need with a promise of the future.

When they broke apart, her breathing had grown heavier. She rested her cheek against his. "You're not going to win every argument with that kind of thing."

He could live with that. "Will I win any?"

"Yes."

Even better. "Then I think you should take me home and have your way with me."

She smiled. "In Britain we call that *shagging.*"

They were finally back on the same page. "I thought you'd never ask."

Keep reading for a sneak peek at

PLAYING DIRTY

by HelenKay Dimon,
the first full-length novel in the
BAD BOYS UNDERCOVER series.

On sale everywhere January 27, 2015.

A Sneak Peek at

PLAYING DIRTY

---

*As an elite Alliance agent—the joint undercover
operation of M16, the British Secret Intelligence Service,
and the CIA—Ford Decker lives for the adrenaline.
But when he befriends sexy property manager Shay
Alexander in hopes of finding her cousin, a known
national security threat, Ford crosses the line,
getting to know her better…in bed.*

*After being burned by her last relationship, Shay wants
to take things slow. Yet she can't keep her hands off
the drop-dead gorgeous hottie who's moved into her
apartment building. So when Ford's identity as an
undercover agent is exposed, his betrayal cuts deep. Shay
never wants to see him again, but Ford can't let her go, not
when her life is still in danger. He will sacrifice everything
to protect her, then be prepared to walk away from the
only woman he's ever loved, even if it breaks him.*

SHAY ALEXANDER HEARD the dueling sounds of off-key humming and a blaring radio as she entered her first-floor condo. She closed the door to shut out the traffic noise and mumble of conversation from people walking by on the sidewalk, but the bad singing remained.

Town houses and stately old homes converted to apartments and condos lined this street in the Dupont Circle area of DC. The Metro sat a few blocks away, and the prime real estate location kept the prices high, which was good since she managed the building and two others for her uncle. She lived alone in the Beaux Arts-style place, which had served as a home to one family in the forties and had since been divided into a twenty-unit complex.

Her small one-bedroom came with the job. The perfect size for a single person, but she'd been fitting two of them in quite nicely on and off for the past three weeks. Which brought her mind back to the not-really-singing thing happening at the back of her condo.

The deep male voice lured her through the family room to the kitchen that ran along the side of the old building. From the doorway she noticed half of the contents of the navy toolbox lay scattered over her tile floor. A can of soda and an open bag of chips sat on the edge of the sink. She didn't know where the snacks came from because buying chips inevitably resulted in her Hoovering the bag in one sitting, so she never stepped one foot into that aisle in the grocery store. That was as far as her chip self-control extended.

The radio, set to deafening, sat on the small table pressed up against the opposite wall. She spied the sneakers next and tiptoed, careful not to tramp down too hard with her boots. There was no need to give away her position. Not when she could steal a moment of looking at him.

Legs, long and lean, stuck out from under her sink. A sliver of bare, trim waist peeked out from the space where his faded jeans and the bottom of what looked like a T-shirt should meet. The unexpected sight of a guy on the floor might scare another woman, but not her. Not those legs, and surely not the impressive male body attached to them.

She winced over a particularly rough note and reached over to turn the radio down. The chips were right there, so she grabbed one. Then two.

"You're back," she said, munching over the salt-and-fat frenzy in her mouth.

Tools clanked, and something thudded. An impressive string of profanity came next. "Shay?"

"Who else?" She still hadn't seen that hot face, with the dark scruff around his chin and those intense green eyes. The guy was of the pure Tall, Dark, and Oh-So-Hot variety. She hated to admit she could stare at him for long periods of time. Look, and totally miss whatever he said.

After rubbing the salt from her fingertips on her jeans, she crouched down, balancing on the balls of her feet, and tried to get a peek at his T-shirt of the day. The graphics ranged from ridiculous to innuendo-filled. None could be classified as appropriate for outside the home. She had no idea where he got them, but she sure enjoyed the ongoing show.

"Hey." He lifted his head and clunked it off the side of a pipe. "Shit."

"Smooth."

He rubbed his temple. "I'm seeing two of you right now."

The scruff was thicker than usual and wasn't that the sexiest thing ever. "You deserved that."

"Hey, I'm fixing your leak." He slid out. The move rolled his shirt up his torso and showed off skin…and muscles…Yeah, forget the T-shirt.

Minor handyman tasks fit in with her job description, but ever since he moved into the two-bedroom across the hall, he'd volunteered to help out. He worked as an IT specialist, handling computer systems for large companies and always on call. But, man, he looked good with a wrench in his hand. She liked him best bare-chested and fixing something.

His smile reeled her in, but she pretended to be immune, or at least a little in control. "You're a plumber now?"

"Want to see my tools?"

The eyebrow wiggle almost did her in. "Wow, that was terrible."

"Yeah, sorry about that." With one hand wrapped around the lip of the sink, he pulled his body up and stood, stopping only for a quick kiss on her mouth. He extended a hand and brought her up beside him before her mind could take in every amazing inch of his six-foot frame. "It was the only line I could think of after a few hours of restless plane sleep and armrest wrangling with the guy in 15B. Give me a few minutes and my moves will catch up to the time zone jumps."

He traveled all the time. In and out, always grabbing a duffel bag and heading off to fix some emergency.

Sometimes texting her at one in the morning to announce he'd gotten back, then knocking on her door to come in for a visit. He'd moved in three weeks ago. The sex started about two days after that.

The relationship—or whatever it was—ran on fast forward from the first day. She'd seen his T-shirt with the piglet playing poker on it, and for some reason her control nosedived. Never mind that it was then October and cold and any sane person would wear a jacket or at least a sweater. He claimed DC was the South and was warm. She guessed that meant he grew up in the Midwest or Vermont or, hell, even Canada. Somewhere cold. Not that he'd shared any part of his past with her…yet. His body, yes. The basic information, no.

She pushed the nagging thought out of her head and ran a finger over the prickly scruff on his chin. "How was the conference?"

"Long and tedious."

"I imagined you hanging out in a bar talking computer code over beers."

He snorted. "More like security measures. Firewalls and rotating IPs."

With that, her already limited interest in the subject of computer tech fizzled out. Him putting his hands on her waist didn't help her focus one bit. She ran her hand over his shirt and smoothed it down over his torso. Today's version featured a cigar-smoking rat.

Of course it did.

"That is something else." The graphic, the abs…the comment worked for both.

He backed her up until her backside balanced against the counter. "Yeah, I've been subjected to some pretty boring lectures and bad conference chicken."

She kicked the wrench rocking under her heel to the side and lifted her arms to circle his neck. "You poor thing."

"And my bed was very cold." He shook his head, even pouted, as he delivered the statement in his most pathetic poor-me tone.

"Are you looking for pity?" She slipped her hand into his hair, as she always did. Something about the length, as if he were growing out a military cut, appealed to her as she wove the softness through her fingers.

His eyebrow lifted. "If that would work."

"You're getting there."

She'd been so sure he was former army—or something—and asked him about it the first week. Nothing in his renter's agreement talked about military service, but she got the vibe. Service members moved in and out of DC all the time. She got the routine and recognized the straight stance and assured conversation. And he had the confident walk and toned body down.

He'd listened to her assessment and laughed it off, insisting his smartass ways would have gotten him kicked out on the first day. She pretty much agreed with that.

"I'm willing to do almost anything to lure you into bed," he said in a heated voice.

"Interesting." And more than a little tempting. After all, he was an expert with that tongue, and not just for talking.

He pulled her in closer, wrapping her in his arms and pressing his chest against hers. "Next time we'll have to schedule in some phone-sex time while I'm gone. Imagine me ordering you to touch yourself. Pretty damn hot."

Her heart did a little jig at the thought. Saying "next time" meant whatever they had wasn't going away. For now, knowing that but little else was enough. Soon she'd need more. "You gotta tone down this sweet-talking or it will go to my head."

Before she could laugh, he lowered his head and treated her to a welcome-home kiss that had her wanting to tie him in a chair to keep from leaving again. Hot and firm, he took control and dragged her under. His hands rubbed up and down her back as his mouth crossed over hers. When that sweet tongue slipped inside and met with hers, she dug her fingernails into his shirt. Almost dug through the cotton to hit skin.

He pulled back just far enough to stare down at her. The room spun, and she held on to his shoulders to keep from falling down as babble filled her brain. "What?"

"I can spit-shine my lines until they're clever, but we both know you're the gatekeeper."

She wasn't exactly sure what he was talking about but she liked the sound of it. "Damn right."

"And I am your sex slave." His voice dipped low until it skidded across her senses.

She clenched her fingers even tighter against his shoulders. Had to clear her throat a few times before finally spitting out a word. "Nice."

Those strong hands slipped down her back to land on her ass. "The green light is totally in your control."

His touch had her stretching up on the tips of her toes to brush her lower body against his. Not her most subtle move, but then nothing about them being together was. They'd shifted from simmering to raging heat from the beginning. Skipped right over the get-to-know-you phase on the way to the bedroom.

She knew about his job and tried to keep a handle on his erratic schedule. His renter's application included his social security number, which led to his impressive credit score and the glowing report from his last landlord in Virginia. The rest remained a mystery...except for the information she found in a few hundred Internet searches trying to make sure he wasn't a wanted serial killer. Or married.

A woman had to be smart about these things. She refused to feel guilty about the dating recon after hearing one horror story too many from her friends. A guy with a hidden wife and an anger complex here. A guy who liked to wear women's bikini underwear over there. Then there were the looking-for-money types. Yeah, no thank you.

Playing coy wasn't her thing, and the attraction between them that sparked on the initial walk through the condo had burst into full flame by the time she handed over the keys. She refused. Two days later he brought pizza over, and they'd been seeing each other ever since.

Seeing as in sex. Lots of sex. The guy might work with computers but he knew his way around a woman's body. Hands, tongue, mouth...Lord.

After a rocky last relationship, the physical play with him and limited dating contact due to his work schedule appealed to her. It didn't matter that the need to know more about him kept picking at her. She'd vowed to turn off her preference for being prepared for anything and just let things unfold without trying to steer them.

In that spirit, she said, "I thought you were blowing out my pipes."

He chuckled in the middle of nibbling on her ear. The sound was so rich and deep, so sexy it hit with the force of a superpower. "I would love to do that, yes."

She felt his arms around her waist with hands caressing her ass and the back of her thighs through her jeans. The dual blast of touching and closeness had her breath stuttering in her chest. She inhaled and caught his scent, the same hint of black pepper she associated with his soap.

Unable to resist his face and that firm chin, she smoothed her fingertip around his mouth, letting the stubble of hair tickle her skin. "You should be resting from your boring conference and long flight."

"That is not what I had in mind when I came over here."

"My pipes, right?" She'd given him a key and the alarm code before he left on his latest trip. He'd been in and out working on the steps to the front door of the building. The argument about needing to get to the supply closet without tracking her down proved compelling. And the idea of him spending his first few hours back in DC fixing the plumbing problem she mentioned on his way out was just about the sexiest damn thing ever.

"Do your pipes need blowing?" He kept a straight face.

She had no idea how. "You make everything sound dirty."

"Give me ten minutes and I'll show you how dirty I can be."

There it was, the flirty talk that drove her doubts away and had her handing over keys even though a little voice inside her head told her to be more careful. But there was no need to fight it. She didn't plan to make him wait or work for it. Those days were behind them, and they had passed fast.

That left only one thing. "I have two words for you."

One of his eyebrows lifted. "Which are?"

She leaned in until her mouth hovered over his. "Green light."

He pulled back as his gaze searched hers. "You sure?"

Since she'd been giving him the go sign pretty much from the beginning and he'd been speeding ahead with her, his hesitation now struck her as odd. But those knowing hands skimming along her sides let her know he was ready when she was.

The answer was now.

"Are you playing hard to get for, like, the first time ever since I've known you?" She pulled him in tighter, rubbing her body against his until his mouth dropped open and a sharp exhale escaped.

His hands clenched against her sides for the briefest of seconds then relaxed again. "Never."

"You know…" She kissed her way down his throat to that delicious spot just above his collarbone. "I think there's something in the bedroom that needs your attention."

His fingers went to the button at the top of her jeans, then the screech of her zipper filled the room. Her mouth covered his just as his fingers slipped inside her underwear. Down and over her. Into her.

She held the back of his neck as her mouth slipped over his again and again. The counter dug into her lower back as his body rocked against hers. None of that mattered. Just his heat and those fingers and his warm breath brushing against her.

When he lifted his head again, he was on the verge of a full-fledged pant. Balancing his forehead against hers, he went to work on the white buttons of her oxford shirt. "What do you need in your bedroom?"

"Just you, Ford Decker."

About the Author

HELENKAY DIMON spent the years before becoming a romance author as a…divorce attorney. Not the usual transition, she knows. Good news is she now writes full time and is much happier. She has sold over thirty novels, novellas, and shorts to numerous publishers. Her nationally bestselling and award-winning books have been showcased in numerous venues, and her books have twice been named "Red-Hot Reads" and excerpted in *Cosmopolitan* magazine. But if you ask her, she'll tell you the best part of the job is never having to wear pantyhose again. You can learn more at her website: www.helenkaydimon.com.

Discover great authors, exclusive offers, and more at hc.com.

Give in to your impulses . . .
Read on for a sneak peek at six brand-new
e-book original tales of romance
from Avon Impulse.
Available now wherever e-books are sold.

AN HEIRESS FOR ALL SEASONS
A Debutante Files Christmas Novella
By Sophie Jordan

INTRUSION
An Under the Skin Novel
By Charlotte Stein

CAN'T WAIT
A Christmas Novella
By Jennifer Ryan

THE LAWS OF SEDUCTION
A French Kiss Novel
By Gwen Jones

SINFUL REWARDS 1
A Billionaires and Bikers Novella
By Cynthia Sax

SWEET COWBOY CHRISTMAS
A Sweet, Texas Novella
By Candis Terry

An Excerpt from

AN HEIRESS FOR ALL SEASONS
A Debutante Files Christmas Novella
by Sophie Jordan

Feisty American heiress Violet Howard swears
she'll never wed a crusty British aristocrat. Will,
the Earl of Moreton, is determined to salvage his
family's fortune without succumbing to a marriage
of convenience. But when a snowstorm strands
Violet and Will together, their sudden chemistry
will challenge good intentions. They're seized by a
desire that burns through the night, but will their
passion survive the storm? Will they realize they've
found a love to last them through all seasons?

His eyes flashed, appearing darker in that moment, the blue as deep and stormy as the waters she had crossed to arrive in this country. "Who are you?"

"I'm a guest here." She motioned in the direction of the house. "My name is V—"

"Are you indeed?" His expression altered then, sliding over her with something bordering belligerence. "No one mentioned that you were an American."

Before she could process that statement—or why he should be told of anything—she felt a hot puff of breath on her neck.

The insolent man released a shout and lunged. Hard hands grabbed her shoulders. She resisted, struggling and twisting until they both lost their balance.

Then they were falling. She registered this with a sick sense of dread. He grunted, turning slightly so that he took the brunt of the fall. They landed with her body sprawled over his.

Her nose was practically buried in his chest. *A pleasant smelling chest.* She inhaled leather and horseflesh and the warm saltiness of male skin.

He released a small moan of pain. She lifted her face to observe his grimace and felt a stab of worry. Absolutely misplaced considering this situation was his fault, but there it was nonetheless. "Are you hurt?"

"Crippled. But alive."

Scowling, she tried to clamber off him, but his hands shot up and seized her arms, holding fast.

"Unhand me! Serves you right if you are hurt. Why did you accost me?"

"Devil was about to take a chunk from that lovely neck of yours."

Lovely? He thinks she is lovely? Or rather her neck is lovely? This bold specimen of a man in front of her, who looks as though he has stepped from the pages of a Radcliffe novel, thinks that plain, in-between Violet is lovely.

She shook off the distracting thought. Virile stable hands like him did not look twice at females like her. No. Scholarly bookish types with kind eyes and soft smiles looked at her. Men such as Mr. Weston who saw beyond a woman's face and other physical attributes.

"I am certain you overreacted."

He snorted.

She arched, jerking away from him, but still he did not budge. His hands tightened around her. She glared down at him, feeling utterly discombobulated. There was so *much* of him—all hard male and it was pressed against her in a way that was entirely inappropriate and did strange, fluttery things to her stomach. "Are you planning to let me up any time soon?"

His gaze crawled over her face. "Perhaps I'll stay like this forever. I rather like the feel of you on top of me."

She gasped.

He grinned then and that smile stole her breath and made all her intimate parts heat and loosen to the consistency of pudding. His teeth were blinding white and straight set against features that were young and strong and much too handsome. And there were his eyes. So bright a blue their brilliance was no less powerful in the dimness of the stables.

Was this how girls lost their virtue? She'd heard the stories and always thought them weak and addle-headed creatures. How did a sensible female of good family cast aside all sense and thought to propriety?

His voice rumbled out from his chest, vibrating against her own body, shooting sensation along every nerve, driving home the realization that she wore nothing beyond her cloak and night rail. No corset. No chemise. Her breasts rose on a deep inhale. They felt tight and aching. Her skin felt like it was suddenly stretched too thin over her bones. "You are not precisely what I expected."

His words sank in, penetrating through the fog swirling around her mind. Why would he expect anything from her? He did not know her.

His gaze traveled her face and she felt it like a touch—a caress. "I shall have to pay closer attention to my mother when she says she's found someone for me to wed."

Violet's gaze shot up from the mesmerizing movement of his lips to his eyes. "Your *mother*?"

He nodded. "Indeed. Lady Merlton."

"Are you . . ." she choked on halting words. *He couldn't be.* "You're the—"

"The Earl of Merlton," he finished, that smile back again, wrapping around the words as though he was supremely amused. As though she were the butt of some grand jest. He was the Earl of Merlton, and she was the heiress brought here to tempt him.

A jest indeed. It was laughable. Especially considering the way he looked. Temptation incarnate. She was not the sort of female to tempt a man like him. At least not without a dowry, and that's what her mother was relying upon.

"And you're the heiress I've been avoiding," he finished.

If the earth opened up to swallow her in that moment, she would have gladly surrendered to its depths.

An Excerpt from

INTRUSION
An Under the Skin Novel
by Charlotte Stein

I believed I would never be able to trust any
man again. I thought so with every fiber of my
being—and then I met Noah Gideon Grant.
Everyone says he's dangerous. But the thing is
. . . I think something happened to him too. I
know the chemistry between us isn't just in my
head. I know he feels it, but he's holding back.
He's made a labyrinth of himself. Now all I
need to do is dare to find my way through.

An Avon Red Novel

He said no sexual contact, and a handshake apparently counts. I should respect that—I do respect that, I swear. I can respect it, no matter how much my heart sinks or my eyes sting at a rejection that isn't a rejection at all.

I can do without. I'm sure I can do without, all the way up to the point where he says words that make my heart soar up, up toward the sun that shines right out of him.

"Kissing is perfectly okay with me," he murmurs, and then, oh, God, then he takes my face in his two good hands, roughened by all the patient and careful fixing he does and so tender I could cry, and starts to lean down to me. Slowly at first, and in these hesitant bursts that nearly make my heart explode, before finally, Lord; finally, yes, finally.

He closes that gap between us.

His lips press to mine, so soft I can barely feel them. Yet somehow, I feel them everywhere. That closemouthed bit of pressure tingles outward from that one place, all the way down to the tips of my fingers and the ends of my toes. I think my hair stands on end, and when he pulls away it doesn't go back down again.

No part of me will ever go back down again. I feel dazed in the aftermath, cast adrift on a sensation that shouldn't have happened. For a long moment I can only stand there in stunned silence, sort of afraid to open my eyes in case the spell is broken.

But I needn't have worried—he doesn't break it. His expression is just like mine when I finally dare to look, full of shivering wonder at the idea that something so small could be so powerful. We barely touched and yet everything is suddenly different. My body is alight. I think his body is alight.

How else to explain the hand he suddenly pushes into my hair? Or the way he pulls me to him? He does it like someone lost at sea, finally seeing something he can grab on to. His hand nearly makes a fist in my insane curls, and when he kisses me this time there is absolutely nothing chaste about it. Nothing cautious.

His mouth slants over mine, hot and wet and so incredibly urgent. The pressure this time is almost bruising, and after a second I could swear I feel his tongue. Just a flicker of it, sliding over mine. Barely anything really, but enough to stun me with sensation. I thought my reaction in the movie theater was intense.

Apparently there's another level altogether—one that makes me want to clutch at him. I need to clutch at him. My bones and muscles seem to have abandoned me, and if I don't hold on to something I'm going to end up on the floor. Grabbing him is practically necessary, even though I have no idea where to grab.

He put his hand in my hair. Does that make it all right to put mine in his? I suspect not, but have no clue where that leaves me. Is an elbow any better? What about his upper arm? His upper arm is hardly suggestive at all, yet I can't quite bring myself to do it. If I do he might break this kiss, and I'm just not ready for that.

I probably won't be ready for that tomorrow. His stubble is burning me just a little and the excitement is making me so shaky I could pass for a cement mixer, but I still want it to carry on. Every new thing he does is just such a revelation— like when he turns a little and just sort of catches my lower lip between his, or caresses my jaw with the side of his thumb.

I didn't think he had it in him.

It could be that he doesn't. When he finally comes up for air he has to kind of rest his forehead against mine for a second. His breathing comes in erratic bursts, as though he just ran up a hill that isn't really there. Those hands in my hair are trembling, unable to let go, and his first words to me blunder out in guttural rush.

"I wasn't expecting that to be so intense," he says, and I get it then. He didn't mean for things to go that way. They just got out of control. All of that passion and urgency isn't who he is, and now he wants to go back to being the real him. He even steps back, and straightens, and breathes long and slow until that man returns.

Now he is the person he wants to be: stoic and cool. Or at least, that's what I think until he turns to leave. He tells me good-bye and I accept it; he touches my shoulder and I process this as all I might reasonably expect in the future. And then just as he's almost gone I happen to glance down, and see something that suggests that the idea of a real him may not be so clear-cut:

The outline of his erection, hard and heavy against the material of his jeans.

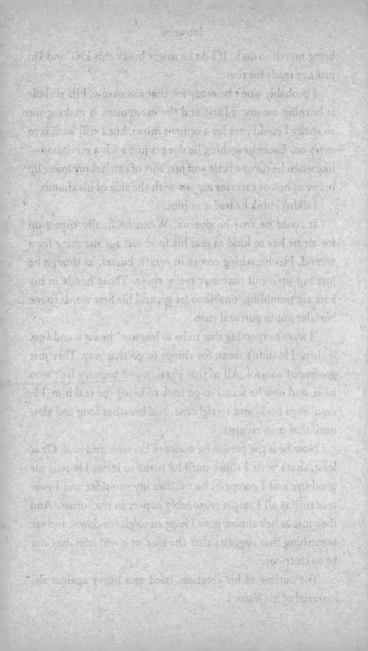

An Excerpt from

CAN'T WAIT
A Christmas Novella
by Jennifer Ryan

(Previously appeared in the anthology
All I Want for Christmas Is a Cowboy)

*Before The Hunted Series, Caleb and Summer
had a whirlwind romance not to be forgotten . . .*

Caleb Bowden has a lot to thank his best friend,
Jack, for—saving his life in Iraq and giving him
a job helping to run his family's ranch. Jack also
introduced Caleb to the most incredible woman
he's ever met. Too bad he can't ask her out. You
do not date your best friend's sister. Summer
and Caleb share a closeness she's never felt
with anyone, but the stubborn man refuses to
turn the flirtatious friendship into something
meaningful. Frustrated and tired of merely
wishing to be happy, Caleb tells Jack how he feels
about Summer. With his friend's help, he plans a
surprise Christmas proposal she'll never forget—
because he can't wait to make her his wife.

Caleb opened his mouth to yell, *Where the hell do you think you're going?*

He snapped his jaw shut, thinking better of it. He couldn't afford to let Jack see how much Summer meant to him. He'd thought he'd kept his need for her under wraps, but the too-observant woman had his number. Over the last few months, the easy friendship they'd shared from the moment he stepped foot on Stargazer Ranch turned into a fun flirtation he secretly wished could turn into something more. The week leading up to Thanksgiving brought that flirtation dangerously close to crossing the line when he walked through the barn door and didn't see her coming out due to the changing light. They crashed into each other. Her sweetly soft body slammed full-length into his and everything in him went hot and hard. Their faces remained close when he grabbed her shoulders to steady her. For a moment, they stood plastered to each other, eyes locked. Her breath stopped along with his and he nearly kissed her strawberry-colored lips to see if she tasted as sweet as she smelled.

Instead of giving in to his baser need, he leashed the beast and gently set her away, walking away without even a single word. She'd called after him, but he never turned back.

Thanksgiving nearly undid him. She'd sat alone in the dining room and all he'd wanted to do was be with her. But how could he? You do not date your best friend's sister. Worse, you do not have dangerous thoughts of sleeping with her, let alone dreaming of a life with a woman kinder than anyone he'd ever met. Just being around her made him feel lighter. She brightened the dark world he'd lived in for too long.

He needed to stay firmly planted on this side of the line. Adhere to the best-bro code. This thing went beyond friendship. Jack was his boss and had saved his life. He owed Jack more than he could ever repay.

"Can you believe her?" Jack pulled him out of his thoughts. He dragged his gaze from Summer's retreating sweet backside.

"Who's the guy?" He kept his tone casual.

Jack glared. "Ex-boyfriend from high school," he said, irritated. "He's home from grad school for the holiday."

"Probably looking for a good time."

Caleb tried not to smile when Jack growled, fisted his hands, and stepped off the curb, following after his sister. He'd counted on Jack's protective streak to allow him to chase Summer himself. Caleb didn't want anyone to hurt her. He sure as hell didn't want her rekindling an old flame with some ex-lover.

He and Jack walked into the park square just as everyone counted down, three, two, one, and the multicolored lights blinked on, lighting the fourteen-foot tree in the center of the huge gazebo, and sparking the carolers to sing "O Christmas Tree."

Tiny white lights circled up the posts and nearby trees, casting a glow over everything. The soft light made Summer's golden hair shine. She smiled with her head tipped back, her bright blue eyes glowing as she stared at the tree.

His temper flared when the guy hooked his arm around her neck and pulled her close, nearly spilling his beer down the front of her. She laughed and playfully shoved him away. The guy smiled and put his hand to her back, guiding her toward everyone's favorite bar. Several other people joined their small group.

Caleb tapped Jack's shoulder and pointed to Summer's back. Her long hair was bundled into a loose braid he wanted to unravel and then run his fingers through the silky strands.

"There she goes."

"What the . . . Let's go get her."

Caleb grabbed Jack's shoulder. "If you go in there and demand she leaves, it'll only embarrass her in front of all her friends. Let's scout the situation. Lie low."

"You're right. She'll only fight harder if we demand she come home. Let's get a beer."

Caleb grimaced. Hell yes, he wanted to drag Summer home, but fought the compulsion.

He did not want to watch her with some other guy.

Why did he torture himself like this?

An Excerpt from

THE LAWS OF SEDUCTION
A French Kiss Novel
by Gwen Jones

In the final fun and sexy French Kiss novel,
sparks fly as sassy lawyer Charlotte Andreko
and Rex Renaud, the COO of Mercier
Shipping, race to clear his name after he's
arrested for a crime he didn't commit.

Center City District Police Headquarters
Philadelphia, PA
Monday, September 29
11:35 PM

In her fifteen years as an attorney, Charlotte had never let anyone throw her off her game, and she wasn't about to let it happen now.

So why was she shaking in her Louboutins?

"Put your briefcase and purse on the belt, keys in the tray, and step through," the officer said, waving her into the metal detector.

She complied, cold washing through her as the gate behind her clanged shut. She glanced over her shoulder, thinking how much better she liked it when her interpretation of "bar" remained figurative.

"Name . . . ?" asked the other cop at the desk.

"Charlotte Andreko."

He ran down the list, checking her off, then held out his hand, waggling it. "Photo ID and attorney card."

She grabbed her purse from the other side of the metal detector and dug into it, producing both. After the officer examined them, he sat back with a smirk. "So you're here for that Frenchie dude, huh? What's he—some kinda big deal?"

She eyed him coolly, hefting her briefcase from the belt. "They're all just clients to me."

"That so?" He dropped his gaze, fingering her IDs. "How come he don't have to sit in a cell? Why'd he get a private room?"

Why are you scoping my legs, you big douche? "It's *your* jail. Why'd you give him one?"

He cocked a brow. "You're pretty sassy, ain't you?"

"And you're wasting my time," she said, swiping back her IDs. *God, it's times like these I really hate men.* "Are you going to let me through or what?"

He didn't answer. He just leered at her with that simpering grin as he handed her a visitor's badge, reaching back to open the next gate.

"Thank you." She clipped it on, following the other cop to one more door at the other side of the vestibule.

"It's late," the officer said, pressing a code into a keypad, "so we can't give you much time."

"I won't need much." After all, how long could it take to say *no fucking way*?

"Then just ring the buzzer by the door when you're ready to leave." When he opened the door and she stepped in, her breath immediately caught at the sight of the man behind it. She clutched her briefcase so tightly she could feel the blood rushing from her fingers.

"*Bonsoir*, Mademoiselle Andreko," Rex Renaud said.

Even with his large body cramped behind a metal table, the Mercier Shipping COO had never looked more imposing—

and, in spite of his circumstances, never more elegant. The last time they'd met had been in Boston, negotiating the separation terms of his company's lone female captain, Dani Lloyd, who had recently become Marcel Mercier's wife. With his cashmere Kiton bespoke now replaced by Gucci black tie, he struck an odd contrast in that concrete room, yet still exuded a coiled and barely contained strength. He folded his arms across his chest as his black eyes fixed on hers, Charlotte getting the distinct impression he more or less regarded her as cornered prey.

All at once the door behind her slammed shut, and her heart beat so violently she nearly called the officer back. Instead she planted her heels and forced herself to focus, staring the Frenchman down. "All right, I'm here," she said *en français*. "Not that I know why."

If there was anything she remembered about Rex Renaud—and he wasn't easy to forget—it was how lethally he wielded his physicality. How he worked those inky eyes, jet-black hair and Greek-statue handsomeness into a kind of immobilizing presence, leaving her weak in the knees every time his gaze locked on hers. Which meant she needed to work twice as hard to keep her wits sharp enough to match his, as no way would she allow him the upper hand.

An Excerpt from

SINFUL REWARDS 1
A Billionaires and Bikers Novella
by *Cynthia Sax*

Belinda "Bee" Carter is a good girl; at least, that's
what she tells herself. And a good girl deserves
a nice guy—just like the gorgeous and moody
billionaire Nicolas Rainer. Or so she thinks,
until she takes a look through her telescope
and sees a naked, tattooed man on the balcony
across the courtyard. He has been watching
her, and that makes him all the more enticing.
But when a mysterious and anonymous text
message dares her to do something bad, she
must decide if she is really the good girl she has
always claimed to be, or if she's willing to risk
everything for her secret fantasy of being watched.

An Avon Red Novella

I'd told Cyndi I'd never use it, that it was an instrument purchased by perverts to spy on their neighbors. She'd laughed and called me a prude, not knowing that I was one of those perverts, that I secretly yearned to watch and be watched, to care and be cared for.

If I'm cautious, and I'm always cautious, she'll never realize I used her telescope this morning. I swing the tube toward the bench and adjust the knob, bringing the mysterious object into focus.

It's a phone. Nicolas's phone. I bounce on the balls of my feet. This is a sign, another declaration from fate that we belong together. I'll return Nicolas's much-needed device to him. As a thank you, he'll invite me to dinner. We'll talk. He'll realize how perfect I am for him, fall in love with me, marry me.

Cyndi will find a fiancé also—everyone loves her—and we'll have a double wedding, as sisters of the heart often do. It'll be the first wedding my family has had in generations.

Everyone will watch us as we walk down the aisle. I'll wear a strapless white Vera Wang mermaid gown with organza and lace details, crystal and pearl embroidery accents, the bodice fitted, and the skirt hemmed for my shorter height. My hair will be swept up. My shoes—

Voices murmur outside the condo's door, the sound piercing my delightful daydream. I swing the telescope upward, not wanting to be caught using it. The snippets of conversation drift away.

I don't relax. If the telescope isn't positioned in the same way as it was last night, Cyndi will realize I've been using it. She'll tease me about being a fellow pervert, sharing the story, embellished for dramatic effect, with her stern, serious dad— or, worse, with Angel, that snobby friend of hers.

I'll die. It'll be worse than being the butt of jokes in high school because that ridicule was about my clothes and this will center on the part of my soul I've always kept hidden. It'll also be the truth, and I won't be able to deny it. I am a pervert.

I have to return the telescope to its original position. This is the only acceptable solution. I tap the metal tube.

Last night, my man-crazy roommate was giggling over the new guy in three-eleven north. The previous occupant was a gray-haired, bowtie-wearing tax auditor, his luxurious accommodations supplied by Nicolas. The most exciting thing he ever did was drink his tea on the balcony.

According to Cyndi, the new occupant is a delicious piece of man candy—tattooed, buff, and head-to-toe lickable. He was completing armcurls outside, and she enthusiastically counted his reps, oohing and aahing over his bulging biceps, calling to me to take a look.

I resisted that temptation, focusing on making macaroni and cheese for the two of us, the recipe snagged from the diner my mom works in. After we scarfed down dinner, Cyndi licking her plate clean, she left for the club and hasn't returned.

Three-eleven north is the mirror condo to ours. I

straighten the telescope. That position looks about right, but then, the imitation UGGs I bought in my second year of college looked about right also. The first time I wore the boots in the rain, the sheepskin fell apart, leaving me barefoot in Economics 201.

Unwilling to risk Cyndi's friendship on "about right," I gaze through the eyepiece. The view consists of rippling golden planes, almost like . . .

Tanned skin pulled over defined abs.

I blink. It can't be. I take another look. A perfect pearl of perspiration clings to a puckered scar. The drop elongates more and more, stretching, snapping. It trickles downward, navigating the swells and valleys of a man's honed torso.

No. I straighten. This is wrong. I shouldn't watch our sexy neighbor as he stands on his balcony. If anyone catches me . . .

Parts 1, 2, 3, 4, and 5 available now!

An Excerpt from

SWEET COWBOY CHRISTMAS
A Sweet, Texas Novella
by Candis Terry

Years ago, Chase Morgan gave up his Texas life
for the fame and fortune of New York City, and
he never planned on coming back—especially
not for Christmas. But when his life is turned
upside down, he finds himself at the door of sexy
Faith Walker's Magic Box Guest Ranch. Chase is
home for Christmas, and it's never been sweeter.

Chase had come up to stand beside her and hand her more ornaments. While most of the influential men who visited the ranch usually reeked of overpowering aftershave, Chase wore the scent of warm man and clean cotton. Tonight, when he'd shown up in a pair of black slacks and a black T-shirt, she'd had to find a composure that had nothing to do with his rescuing her.

She'd taken a fall all right.

For him.

Broken her own damn rules is what she'd done. Hadn't she learned her lesson? Men with pockets full of change they threw around like penny candy at a parade weren't the kind she could ever be interested in.

At least never again.

Trouble was, Chase Morgan was an extremely sexy man with bedroom eyes and a smile that said he could deliver on anything he'd promise in that direction. Broad shoulders that confirmed he could carry the weight of the world if need be. And big, capable hands that had already proven they could catch her if she fell.

He was trouble.

And she had no doubt she was in trouble.

Best to keep to the subject of the charity work and leave the drooling for some yummy, untouchable movie star like Chris Hemsworth or Mark Wahlberg.

Discreetly, she moved to the other side of the tree and hung a pinecone Santa on a higher branch. "We also hold a winter fund-raiser, which is what I'm preparing for now."

"What kind of fund-raiser?" he asked from right beside her again, with that delicious male scent tickling her nostrils.

"We hold it the week before Christmas. It's a barn dance, bake sale, auction, and craft fair all rolled into one." She escaped to the other side of the tree, but he showed up again, hands full of dangling ornaments. "Last year we raised $25,000. I'd like to top that this year if possible."

"You must have a large committee to handle all that planning."

She laughed.

Dark brows came together over those green eyes that had flashes of gold and copper near their centers. "So I gather you're not just the receptionist-slash–tree decorator."

"I have a few other talents I put to good use around here."

"Now you've really caught my interest."

To get away from the intensity in his gaze, she climbed up the stepstool and placed a beaded-heart ornament on the tree. She could only imagine how he probably used that intensity to cut through the boardroom bullshit.

As a rule, she never liked the clientele to know she was the sole owner of the ranch. Even though society should be living in this more open-minded century, there were those who believed it was still a man's world.

"Oh, it's really nothing that special," she said. "Just some odds and ends here and there."

When she came down the stepstool, his hands went to her waist to provide stability. At least that's what she told herself, even after those big warm palms lingered when she'd turned around to face him.

"Fibber," he said while they were practically nose to nose.

"I beg your pardon?"

"You know what I do for a living, Faith? How I've been so successful? I read people. I come up with an idea, then I read people for how they're going to respond. Going into a pitch, I know whether they're likely to jump on board or whether I need to go straight to plan B."

His grip around her waist tightened, and the fervor with which he studied her face sent a shiver racing down her spine. There was nothing threatening in his eyes or the way his thumbs gently caressed the area just above the waistband of her Wranglers.

Quite the opposite.

"You have the most expressive face I've ever seen," he declared. "And when you're stretching the truth, you can't look someone in the eye. Dead giveaway."

"And you've known me for what? All of five minutes?" she protested.

One corner of his masculine lips slowly curved into a smile. "Guess that's just me being presumptuous again."

Everything female in Faith's body awakened from the death sleep she'd put it in after she'd discovered the man she'd been just weeks away from marrying, hadn't been the man she'd thought him to be at all.

"Looks like we're both a little too trigger-happy in the jumping-the-gun department," she said, while deftly extricating herself from his grasp even as her body begged her to stay put.

"Maybe."

Backing away, she figured she'd tempted herself enough for one night. Best they get dinner over with before she made some grievous error in judgment she'd never allow herself to forget.

She clapped her hands together. "So . . . how about we get to that dinner?"

"Sounds great." His gaze wandered all over her face and body. "I'm getting hungrier by the second."

Whoo boy.